SECRETS OF HER FORBIDDEN KNIGHT

Ella Matthews

MILLS & BOON

First published in Great Britain 2022
by Mills & Boon, an imprint of HarperCollins*Publishers* Ltd,
1 London Bridge Street, London, SE1 9GF

www.harpercollins.co.uk

HarperCollins*Publishers*
1st Floor, Watermarque Building,
Ringsend Road, Dublin 4, Ireland

MIX
Paper from
responsible sources
FSC® C007454

This book is produced from independently certified FSC™ paper
to ensure responsible forest management.
For more information visit www.harpercollins.co.uk/green.

Printed and Bound in Spain using 100% Renewable Electricity
at CPI Black Print, Barcelona

To the best son in the world, Jacob.

Chapter One

South Coast of England, winter 1337

Johanne signalled to Gemel to slow his horse as she brought her own to a stop. The path was narrow at this point, trees tightly packed along its edge, and a bend up ahead meant visibility was poor. It was the perfect place for an ambush.

'There's something on the path up ahead,' she called to Gemel, who was riding behind her. 'The rain's making it difficult to see but there's a long black mound that wasn't there this morning, blocking the route.'

'What do you think it is?'

'It looks like a body but I'm not sure.'

'I should go first, mistress.'

Johanne heard Gemel's horse's hooves shuffle as he prepared to move past her but she shook her head. She was the leader and he was her steward. She couldn't afford to show any weakness, not even in front of Gemel, not even when tensions were high as the country edged closer to war with France and there was no telling what traps lay in wait for the unwary. Not even when an attempt on her life had already been made. If there was one thing she had learned from her late husband, it was that the leader always had to be in control: nobody else.

'Mistress, if it's a body we should head back and find an alternative route.'

Gemel made to turn his horse, but Johanne held up a hand to stay him. The lump was unmoving…if it was a person perhaps they were already dead. A murder so close to Brae was not to be taken lightly. 'I'm going to take a closer look.'

Rain dripped off the edge of Johanne's hood as she edged Heled forward, ignoring Gemel's muted grumbling. She understood her steward's concerns but if there was a threat to her castle's safety it was better she found out now.

Up close, it was clear the shape was a body, a male and a large one at that. She peered down at him as rain hammered down, splashing onto his cheeks and running off his face. He was deathly still but she thought she saw the slight rise and fall of his chest.

'It's a man,' she called back to her steward. 'And a wealthy one going by his clothing. I don't think he's dead. It looks like he's breathing but it's hard to tell from up here.'

She made to get down from her horse.

'We should ride on.' The fear in Gemel's voice was evident now. 'This could be another ambush.'

Johanne twisted around in her saddle, trying to peer through the trees lining the path, but it was impossible in the driving rain. There was no sound amongst the undergrowth; it appeared even the birds had taken refuge from the storm.

'He's probably a drunkard. Nobody will miss him,' muttered Gemel but Johanne was no longer listening to anything her steward said. She could no more leave someone to die alone than she could kill an innocent. She slipped down from her horse.

'Mistress, I don't like this. Get back on Heled and we'll away.'

As Gemel didn't like much, Johanne had no problem ignoring his comment. Even so she kept one hand on her horse and moved slowly forward, prepared at any moment to ride away if this turned out to be a trap.

She reached the body. The man was breathing but only just. She nudged his ribs with the tip of her boot. He didn't stir. She prodded harder; still nothing.

She crouched down. This close she could see the start of a beard on a rugged face. Thick, dark hair was plastered to his forehead and his cloak was soaked through. This was not someone who had recently lain down here in the hope of unsuspecting travellers coming past; he had been lying here awhile. The buckle at his throat was silver, the sign of a wealthy merchant perhaps?

She leaned nearer. Yes, he was definitely breathing but his lips were a worrying shade of blue. She reached out a hand and lightly brushed her fingers over his forehead.

A hand clamped around her arm. The grip so tight it burned against her skin. She gasped and tried to tug herself free but the hold was too strong.

Two dark eyes glared at her beneath bushy eyebrows.

'Angel,' croaked the man before his eyes fluttered shut and his hand dropped to his side.

Johanne rubbed her wrist where the stranger had held her.

'Mistress...' Gemel was down from his horse, striding towards her with his dagger half drawn from its scabbard. 'Are you hurt?'

'No.' She brushed the stranger's forehead again, feeling oddly protective. 'He didn't want to hurt me. I think he thought he'd died and gone to heaven.'

Gemel snorted, sheathing his weapon, although he kept his hand resting on the hilt. 'A sorry place paradise would be if you were the person greeting souls on their arrival.'

Johanne smiled at Gemel's joke. He was right though. The man must be in the grip of a fever if he mistook her for an angelic being. She'd been compared to the devil more than once since her husband's death. Not that she minded. In a world ruled by men, it didn't hurt to have a strong image and it was one she'd spent the last few years cultivating. Her reputation was of a much more powerful woman than the weak one she'd been when she was married. It was an image she did not want to relinquish now she had gained it, even if it often felt draining to live behind such a mask.

'We must take him with us.'

Gemel didn't argue this time. Now that they were closer to the body, it was obvious the man was injured and no threat to either of them, and even Gemel couldn't resist helping a man in need.

'We'll put him over Maldwyn,' said Johanne. 'I don't think Heled will cope with the size of him.'

Gemel bent down and hefted the man by his shoulders. 'Aye, but he's as heavy as a draught horse.'

Johanne laughed softly as she picked up the man's legs. They were as solid as tree trunks. She gripped the muscled calves tightly, still determined not to show any weakness, physically or mentally.

The man didn't stir as they hefted him sideways over Maldwyn. Even Gemel's horse staggered under the weight, but the stallion had been trained well and didn't try to throw off his unwelcome burden.

'What's this?'

Johanne turned away from the man and looked where Gemel was pointing. A thin rope had been tied across the path, difficult to see in the pouring rain. It would be especially hard from atop a horse.

'It's a trap.' Johanne moved towards it. 'There's blood on it here.' She glanced back at the man. 'It's not his; he's not bleeding. Perhaps he was on a horse and it ran into it. It would be enough to throw anyone off, although perhaps not to knock them unconscious.' She stood and looked about but there was no sign of an injured animal in the dense treeline.

'We don't have time to look for the horse,' said Gemel. Johanne agreed. If this was indeed a trap, those who set it could be nearby. She glanced back towards the treeline; a cold shiver ran down her spine. 'Do you think this is Morcant's doing? Is there any way he could have found out I would be on this path today?'

'Aye, I think we need to be wary, mistress.' Gemel reached down and cut the rope with his dagger. 'We should leave the man here. He could be in league with Morcant.'

'Or he has been injured because Morcant was only expecting us on this path today.'

'That doesn't make his injuries your fault, mistress.'

'If we leave him, he will die.' She would not

leave the stranger here, not when she could do something to help him.

Gemel gave a tight nod. 'We had best get on then.'

'Brae needs more manpower,' said Johanne as they resumed their journey with Gemel leading his horse. 'A man with this one's size could be a good asset.'

Johanne couldn't make out Gemel's response over the pouring rain but from the set of his shoulders she could tell he didn't agree with her. He'd no doubt want the stranger gone as soon as he was healed. But then, it wasn't up to Gemel who lived at Castle Brae. Ever since her domineering husband had died all decisions regarding the small stronghold were down to her and she had no intention of that changing. Not until her son reached his majority and she could hand him his legacy. Until then, she would do whatever was needed to make sure Brae was as strong as it could be, and if that meant being a ruthless leader, then so be it. She had watched Badon and learned from him that the best way to maintain power was to always appear to be in complete control. She was not in her role to make friends, only to form alliances with those who could help her cause.

They were not far from Brae when they'd picked up the stranger, but the relentless rain had turned the paths into rivers of mud, making the journey painfully slow. The man didn't wake, not even when Gemel slipped, cursing loudly as he fell. After that, Johanne joined Gemel on the ground, helping to lead both horses over the treacherous terrain.

Johanne would never admit it but by the time they arrived back at Brae she almost regretted picking up the stranger. There was no inch of her body that wasn't soaking wet, her skin feeling as if she had bathed for too long. She wanted nothing more than to head to her chamber and divest herself of her clothing and then warm herself by the fire, but as the castle's leader she had to stay until arrangements were made for the stranger.

'We'll put him in the room below mine,' she told Gemel as they brought their horses to a stop in the compact courtyard.

'Are you sure that's wise?'

'It is the only chamber with a lock on the outside.'

Gemel grunted, clearly displeased at having

the stranger sleeping so close to his mistress when most of the inhabitants slept in the Great Hall, but he didn't argue. Perhaps he was exhausted. It had been a strenuous walk, guiding the horses along the muddy paths, and Gemel had passed his fortieth summer, his age showing in the deep lines around his mouth. She should stop relying on him so much, but it was hard. There were very few people she trusted, and he was one of them, and even then she didn't tell him everything. She didn't want him to know the secrets of her heart. So long as he thought her strong, that was all that mattered.

Between them they managed to get the man across the courtyard and into the small keep. Johanne's muscles strained. She held her grip even though she was desperate to let go of her heavy cargo.

'Send Mary to me with some dry blankets for him,' she said when they had finally placed him on the straw mattress.

'You shouldn't be alone with him. We know nothing of his temperament. It would be nothing for him to crush you.'

'Gemel, the man cannot move. I am in no danger.' Johanne drew herself to her full height and stared down at her steward, willing him to do her bidding.

She was hanging on to control of Brae by a thin thread. One defiance could set the whole thing tumbling.

The moment stretched. Johanne's heart began to race. Could this be the time when it all came tumbling down around her? She was always expecting it, always waiting for someone to defy her orders. Badon had never given her any respect and it constantly amazed her that the castle inhabitants gave it to her now. She knew it was only a matter of time before someone saw through her bravado but to lose control over something so simple would be humiliating.

She held Gemel's gaze. She would not give in, not now, not ever.

Eventually he nodded and turned away from her.

She held her stance until she could no longer hear his footsteps. When she was sure she was alone apart from the unconscious man, she let out a long breath, her fingers trembling with the enormity of what she had done.

Gemel was right. If the man woke and turned out to be aggressive, he could snap her neck in an instant. But the man had barely stirred during the whole trip and, looking at him passed out on the mattress, she doubted he would do so now.

Her steward had come close to defying her today. She could tell in the long hesitant moments. And yes, that had been down to his concerns about her safety, and yes, she understood that, but Gemel would not have wavered if she had been Badon. Badon would not have tolerated the hesitancy for a moment. He would have stripped Gemel of his stewardship if Gemel had shown even a hint of disobeying his orders. Johanne was not as ruthless as that, even though she put on a show emulating some of Badon's more tolerable leadership strategies. She could never be as hot-headed as Badon, never humiliate or put down a person in order to get them to bend to her will. Even so, she couldn't allow any insubordination. Sometimes, getting the balance right was exhausting.

She couldn't keep juggling things like this. She needed to do something to shore up her control, something that would make no one doubt her ability to rule. The problem was the options open to her were limited and some of them were distasteful and reminded her too forcibly of her late husband.

No matter. She would worry about it later. Now, she had the stranger to contend with.

She crouched down at the edge of the mattress. The man hadn't stirred since they had dropped him there. In the quietness of the room she could hear his breathing. It was steady but shallow. She touched his forehead. He was still icy cold but he didn't appear to be bleeding from any wounds; if she could keep him from catching a fever he would probably live.

She ran her gaze over the rest of his body. She'd been right when she'd thought his clothes were that of a wealthy man. The material of his cloak was thick and of expensive quality and the binding at his throat was a silver clasp intricately decorated with birds.

She undid it, the soft bristles of his neck brushing against the backs of her fingers. She peeled the material back. Beneath the cloak, fine clothes clung to him like a second skin, the muscles of his chest clearly defined.

She swallowed.

It wasn't that she hadn't seen a man's body before. Badon had been proud of his naked torso, not missing any opportunity to show his strength off to the world by stripping off and parading his muscles whenever the opportunity arose.

Since his death, she'd seen men in the court-yard stripped to their waists as they worked and not spared them a second glance. But then, not one of them had the defined muscles of this stranger. When he was fit and well, he must be a powerful sight to behold.

She reached out a hand to trace the contours of his chest before snatching her hand back. Undressing him so that he didn't die from the cold was acceptable, stroking him was not.

She jumped as the chamber door banged open. She stood quickly as Mary bustled into the room and dumped a pile of kindling into the hearth.

The maid hurried over to the mattress and peered down at the stranger. 'Ooh, he's a hand-some one. He'd warm a bed something lovely and no mistake.'

Johanne resisted the urge to cover the stranger up. 'Light the fire please, Mary.'

Even though Johanne had been admiring the man's physique only moments before, Mary's comments about his looks rankled. She wanted the young maid gone from the room which, she realised as she began to unpick the wet ties of the stranger's tunic, was absurd. Just because she'd saved his life did not mean she had a hold over him. 'Once you've got the flames going, come and help me get him undressed. He weighs as much as all the hay in the barn put together.'

'Right you are, mistress.'

Perhaps Johanne's idea of keeping the well-built man to help out at Brae was not such a good one after all. Perhaps she should get rid of him as soon as possible. Even unconscious he was causing her to act unlike herself, to snap at her workers and to make irrational decisions. She would give the matter some serious consideration if the man ever woke up. If he died before the night was over, her decision would be made for her.

Alewyn woke slowly, his head pounding and his whole body aching as if he'd fought an entire army of Frenchmen.

His forehead itched but his limbs were too heavy to scratch the sensation away.

'Are you awake?' a female voice whispered.

He stopped breathing. What had happened last night? He didn't remember bedding anyone. Had he been drinking and lost control of his actions? But no. He'd been on his way somewhere. Benedictus, his leader, had sent him. There was a mission and that meant there was no time for drinking or bedding or enjoyment of any sort. Not if he was to fulfil his promise to himself.

'I can see your eyelids flickering. Do you know where you are?' The voice continued to question him but he had no strength to answer. 'Do you know what happened before you were injured?'

No, he definitely hadn't bedded this woman. He would never go for someone so persistent. Alewyn's eyelids were heavy and refused his commands to open.

'Do you know what you were doing on the path?'

Alewyn licked his lips. Perhaps if he answered her she would stop. 'No… I don't…' His voice sounded croaky, as if he had imbibed too many ales. He knew nothing about the path about which she was talking.

'You don't remember anything?'

Alewyn shook his head. Why wouldn't this woman stop talking and give him a moment to think?

'No… I…' He wanted to say that he knew who he was; he just couldn't remember how he found himself to be in the position he was in now. He wanted to ask where he was and explain that he knew nothing about paths and ask why his body ached so much. But his thoughts were swirling and nothing made sense. Words failed him and the world went black again.

Moments or days later, Alewyn woke again. He lay still, waiting for his questioner to begin, but all was silent. His lids were still heavy but he managed to force them open. Above him was a high, stone ceiling suggesting he was in a castle and not a peasant's hut, although the mattress beneath him was not comfortable. Perhaps he was a prisoner; it was hard to tell.

His body screamed as he pushed himself up onto his elbows. Blinking, he took in his surroundings. The chamber was small but clean with a fire burning in the grate. Heavy blankets covered him, soft against his skin.

He froze.

Pushing back the covers, he glanced down at himself. Someone had divested him of his clothes. Purple bruises covered almost all his skin; no wonder he was in so much pain. Had there been a fight? He didn't think so. Surely, he would remember. But then, he'd not lost a fight since he'd reached adulthood. Not even when five men had jumped him from behind. It had been them who'd ended up bloodied and bruised, not him.

The way his mysterious questioner had spoken to him suggested she had no idea what had happened to him either. Although she could be lying. He groaned. Thinking was not easy when his head pounded so violently.

He squinted at the rest of the room but there was no sign of his clothes. The chamber was empty save for the mattress he was lying on.

Well, if they, whoever *they* were, thought nudity would keep him prisoner in this chamber, they were mistaken.

He made to push himself fully upright but his muscles screamed in protest.

What on earth had happened to him and why couldn't he remember anything about it?

Chapter Two

The door to the chamber creaked open. A woman, all coppery curls and willowy limbs, stepped through the gap and moved quickly into the chamber. There was an urgency to her step as if she were rushing to or from something very important.

'You're awake. How are you feeling? You look like you've taken a bit of a pummelling.'

Alewyn blinked. He recognised the breathy questioning as belonging to his persistent inquisitor, the one who wanted to know everything when he was barely even conscious. As she came closer, he thought he recognised her from somewhere, as if he had seen those blue eyes and high forehead before, but he couldn't place her. It was so frustrating, not remembering everything. It was as if he were reaching through fog trying to get a grasp of something solid only for it to slip away before he could hold on tight.

The woman arrived at his side and placed a tankard near his head. 'I thought you might be thirsty.'

Spying the liquid, his throat began to burn. He hadn't realised just how much he was in need of a drink until now but he wasn't sure he could lift the flagon to his mouth. He glanced at the woman. She was watching him with speculation. No, he wasn't going to attempt it in front of her. He was not going to reveal his weakness, not before he knew whether she was his friend or his enemy.

She turned away from him and made her way over to the hearth, stretching her fingers out towards the warmth of the flickering fire. Alewyn watched her for a moment. She was tall, taller than most women, but still shorter than him. Her dress was practical but well-made, and beneath it he could make out gentle curves. Curves that would fit perfectly in his hands. His body stirred and he frowned at the unwelcome movement even as he was pleased that at least one aspect of him still worked.

It was of no matter. He was in no position

to bed a woman and, even if he was and she was interested, he would not do it. Despite his obvious physical attraction, she was not his type. His way of life was often harsh and brutal. Whenever he sought out female companionship, it was with a softly spoken woman, someone who was gentle and soothing. Everything this woman was not. Even now, though she was still, she appeared to be vibrating with an energy she could barely contain.

He knew it was only a matter of moments before she began talking again. He watched as she inhaled, ready to speak. Before she could begin her interrogation, he blurted out, 'Am I a prisoner?'

She spun to face him, her jaw dropping open until she snapped it shut. 'No. Why would you think that?' She made her way back to him. 'Have you done something you shouldn't have? Is that why you were lying there?'

What was she talking about? She appeared to be talking in riddles; it was beyond frustrating. Thankfully his irritation killed his unwanted attraction. 'Where exactly was I lying?'

'On the path.'

'What path?'

'The one leading here.'

Was she being deliberately infuriating not answering his questions? Where exactly was this path and why did she think he'd been lying on it? He'd never intentionally lie down anywhere unless it was in a secure fortress, but if he'd been attacked no one would have left him alive. He was too dangerous. None of this made any sense.

'Do you need some help with the drink?'

He looked up. She'd moved closer to him while he was thinking and the scent of something floral reached him. Now she was so close, he could reach out and touch her.

'No. I don't need any help.' She stood watching him, waiting for him to move. Despite not wanting to show weakness, he was so thirsty he didn't think he could wait until she left him alone. He pushed himself upright; only his years of training stopped him from groaning out loud. He'd be damned if he couldn't take a sip without help, even if he didn't mind the thought of those slender fingers on his body.

He managed not to grunt in pain as he lifted the drink to his lips but it was a hard-won victory.

'What happened to you?'

He put the tankard down. 'Do you ever stop asking questions?'

'Only when they're answered.'

She held his gaze, no sign of fear in the depths of her eyes, which was unusual. Granted, he was lying on his back, naked, covered in bruises and without a clue as to how he had got there, but he could still snap her like a twig. Or at least he assumed he could. It would hurt him to move, what with every muscle and bone screaming in agony, but he was certain he could best her in a fight, even if she had ten guards outside the door ready to protect her should she say the word. He'd been trained to win any skirmish almost from the moment of his birth. He'd had many injuries, far worse than he was experiencing right now, and he'd always come back fighting.

She should be afraid of him; most people were. They saw his size and immediately guessed at his capability. This woman should be the same. She wasn't to know the depth of his incapacity right at this moment, and yet, she seemed totally calm in his presence.

She knelt beside him, not seeming to mind her skirts on the dusty floor. Once more, he was struck by how familiar she seemed. 'Have we met before?'

'No.' She shook her head, a few more coppery curls escaping from her braid. 'At least not before yesterday when we found you.'

'We?'

'Gemel and I?'

So, she was married. Of course she was. A beauty like her wouldn't be unwed, especially at her age. Alewyn guessed she must be in her mid-twenties. Odd that her husband would allow her to be alone in a chamber with a man who could so easily overpower her. Still, he supposed there may be many men outside the chamber door listening to what he said. Perhaps her husband thought a pretty face would make him talk. It wouldn't.

'Why are you staring?'

Heat washed over Alewyn. He'd been so busy gazing at her he had forgotten she could see exactly what he was doing. He lifted the tankard to his lips and took another sip, hiding his face until he was sure the colour had gone from his skin. 'You look familiar,' he hedged.

She shrugged. 'Maybe you remember me from yesterday. You opened your eyes briefly.' For some reason her cheeks pinkened and her gaze flickered away from him. She took a deep breath. 'Do you remember who you are yet?'

Yes, he did remember. He was Alewyn Monceaux, one of King Edward's four most trusted knights and second son of one of the most influential barons in the Kingdom but he didn't know who she was and until he did… 'I'm afraid my memory is sketchy.' This was not an outright lie. 'Perhaps I will remember when I see my belongings.' Maybe they would give him a clue as to why he was alone and away from Windsor without the backup of his fellow knights. It was very rare for him to travel alone. He prayed nothing terrible had befallen his brothers-in-arms. If he was lying here while his fellow knights were in danger, he would never forgive himself.

'You didn't have any belongings.'

His heart stopped. That didn't sound right. He never travelled without, at the very least, his sword. She must be keeping something from him; she had to be lying. But she was gazing right at him, her blue eyes guileless. Either she was an extremely good liar or she was telling the truth. 'Nothing? Are you sure?'

'Yes, there was nothing around you. You were lying across the path on your back. There was no sign you had been in a fight but you were unconscious. When I undressed you I saw that you were covered in bruises, so maybe you had been in an altercation and you lost.'

Unlikely. He hadn't lost a fight in years. Wait… Did she just say…? But surely not… 'You undressed me?'

He watched as a blazing red rushed across her face. She turned away from him and an answering heat spread across his own face. He'd blushed twice now in the last few moments, which was beyond ridiculous. He was never embarrassed or, at least, he normally managed to hide it if he ever experienced the emotion.

She recovered first. 'Well, you couldn't stay in the soaking wet clothes. You'd have caught your death and I'd have had the trouble of burying you. Your clothes are drying.' She stood abruptly and made for the door. 'I'll check on them, but they were completely soaked through, so I don't hold out much hope. I'll bring you something to wear in the meantime.' She looked back at him. 'Although I'm not sure there'll be anything to find that's quite your size.'

Good to know that she had realised how big

he was but still didn't seem afraid of him. She continued to walk towards the door.

'Are you sure I am not a prisoner, mistress?'

'Of course not.'

He couldn't see her face, so he couldn't be sure, but he thought she might be telling the truth, which made the situation even stranger. Why keep him in a room without his own clothes when he wasn't being held captive? And then there was the bruising. Could it be that her husband had inflicted it on him and that's why he wasn't showing himself to Alewyn? If only he could remember what had happened.

The door creaked as she pulled it open.

'Where am I?' he asked before she disappeared.

She turned to face him. 'Castle Brae on the south coast of England.' She stood for a moment, watching him as if waiting for a reaction.

He held himself still even as memories hit him like a punch to the gut.

Seemingly satisfied that the name meant nothing to him, she nodded and turned to go, the door closing softly behind her. He listened intently but there was no sound of a lock turning, so perhaps he really wasn't a prisoner. Although what sort of person trusted a strange man in their stronghold? There had to be guards outside the chamber; to leave him unguarded made no sense.

He sighed. There was so much he didn't know but the things that he did were not good.

He pushed himself off the mattress, stifling a groan as his insides screamed. He still couldn't recall how he had come to be lying across a path without his belongings or his horse, but he remembered why he was in this part of the country and he knew he was in deep trouble.

He staggered over to the fireplace and dropped to his haunches in front of it. The flames warmed his skin even as a chill swept through his body.

Benedictus, who was not only the leader of the King's Knights but also his older brother, would be furious if he could see him now, naked, beaten and clueless. Second only to his father's anger, who would see it as evidence that his second son was every bit the disappointment he'd always believed.

The only positive thing Alewyn could dredge up from this sorry mess was that he *had* set out on the journey alone and, as far as he knew, his knights-in-arms were fine and not relying on him for a rescue.

Alewyn dropped his head into his hands and groaned. He'd long assumed he was a member of the King's Knights because he was so closely related to their leader. Their parents had wanted two sons to hold prestigious roles in King Edward's court and it didn't come much higher than the King's Knights. Benedictus was cut from the same cloth as his parents. The Monceaux name had to be powerful, and what was more powerful than the elite group of warriors who protected the King.

It was true that Alewyn's intimidating size and skill with the sword made him a formidable opponent, but he did not have other skills, not like the other knights in the exclusive order. Will had his analytical mind, Theo his ability to read people and Benedictus had the command needed to lead them. None of them had his size, but they could all fight as well as Alewyn. Alewyn did not have anything special about him, not like the others.

He'd hoped that this mission would finally prove he was meant to belong, that he was worthy of his place in the group of men who protected the King's interests. But no. He'd already unwittingly botched his charge before he'd made any progress.

He groaned again. He'd failed before he'd truly begun. Instead of controlling circumstances as he should have done, he was wounded, naked and without significant parts of his memory. And, to make matters worse, he was all of those things *and* he was in the castle of the widowed Lady Brae.

He knew now why she seemed familiar. Her likeness had been described to him in detail before he had left. Her husband had died some time ago and the beautiful widow was said to be vivacious, cunning and treacherous.

She was also the very woman Benedictus had sent him to investigate.

Johanne stood outside the chamber, the stranger's clothes clutched against her chest. Her knees were trembling. She let out a long breath, hoping to calm her nerves. She couldn't understand why she was acting like this. She was a grown woman, a widow and a mother and in charge of a small but significant stronghold. She was not some silly girl waiting for her first kiss from a handsome squire.

If the man saw his belongings, remembered

who he was and left, she was no worse off than she'd ever been. And if he didn't and decided to stay, then the increased manpower would be useful for Brae. No, it would be more than useful. It would be a godsend. Many men had stayed with her after the death of Badon, but they were the ones with families. Men who were getting older and who were not as strong as they once were. The more able-bodied men had left, seeking a stronghold with a male leader, one who would lead them to war, where they might find death or glory.

Johanne was left with a depleted workforce and a castle that urgently needed upkeep. Despite all that, she had to keep Brae safe. Her young son's inheritance hung on her staying in control until he was old enough to take over. She could do it; she *would* do it.

This winter had been hard and some of Brae's defences had crumbled, leaving holes in the walls. Work on repairing them was slow. A man of the stranger's strength would help speed that up but the work would get done without him. Finding out whether he would stay or not was not a move to be agonised over, but she still didn't move from the corridor; she wasn't quite ready to confront him.

Her fingers stroked over the stranger's ornate clasp. A man with this sort of wealth would have connections. Someone important would be missing him. Perhaps to keep the stranger at Brae would invite a scrutiny she desperately wanted to avoid. Perhaps she should give him his clothes and send him on his way. Her troubles were not his.

She shook her head. Enough. She was irritating herself with her indecision. She would return the man's clothes and offer him refuge, and if he didn't want to take it, that was… well…that was fine. It did not matter to her.

Without knocking she strode into the chamber, coming to a complete stop when she caught sight of him.

The man was crouched in front of the fire, light from the flames flickering over his skin.

Everything she'd planned to say fled from her mind. Her breath caught as the moment seemed to stretch into eternity. His body was breathtaking.

He stood, his muscles rippling as he turned to face her. She forced her gaze to stay on his face and not to drop any lower. He raised an eyebrow and the moment broke.

'Your clothes.' She thrust the bundle to him,

her mind unable to conjure up a coherent sentence.

'Thank you.' His fingers brushed the backs of her hands and she jolted as sensation rippled through her. She had never felt anything like that before. She touched the base of her throat; her pulse thundered erratically beneath her fingertips.

He dumped the bundle on the mattress and returned to his place by the fire, keeping the front of his body facing the warmth.

She frowned. 'Aren't you going to put them on?'

'Not right now.'

'But I can't talk to you like that.' She gestured to his naked body, the sight of which seemed to be playing havoc with her own.

'You've been talking to me just fine. Besides, haven't you seen it all before? You were the one who undressed me, I recall.'

'I… But… You…' Her words were all jumbled up and she couldn't seem to find the right ones to say. Was that why he was doing it? Did he think she would be intimidated by his nakedness? Well, she wouldn't. She would just have to pretend that she wasn't affected by all the muscles she could see at the edge of her vision.

She squared her shoulders. 'Have you re-membered anything yet?'

He shook his head slowly. 'Not yet, mis-tress.'

'Hmm.' She folded her arms across her chest. 'If you don't have your memory, what do you plan to do?'

'I plan to… I mean, I assumed…' He half turned to face her and she noticed a slight tinge of red crossing his cheeks. Good. She was pleased she wasn't the only one uncom-fortable with the situation. She pushed aside the errant thought that, for a mountain of a man, he was adorable when he blushed. She wasn't here to form attachments. A man of his size would be used to dominating others. She would not live like that again, never be at the mercy of someone who could control her whenever they wanted. Never would she bow to someone else's commands. She was in control and not this stranger. She was here to work out how his presence at Brae could best be used to her advantage and nothing else.

He cleared his throat. 'Mistress, may I stay here until I regain my memory, or someone comes to find me? I hope that I am not all alone in the world, although I suppose I could be.'

Johanne managed to hide her triumphant smile. This was exactly what she'd been hoping for, though she didn't want him to know that. 'Of course you may, although you'll be expected to work. Brae is not so wealthy that I can support guests who do nothing all day.'

He nodded briskly. 'I would expect nothing less.'

Perfect. With shoulders like his, he'd be a huge asset. Although perhaps she should mention… 'You'll have to wear clothes.'

His lips twitched and Johanne's heart fluttered strangely. 'Aye, mistress. I suppose I will.'

She waited but he still didn't move towards the mattress and his pile of clothing. Johanne realised she couldn't very well stand there and wait; that was too odd, and besides, he was to be one of her men now. She couldn't gaze at him like a silly maiden who still thought the world was a kind place and that men were heroes who didn't want women to submit to their decree.

'I'll leave you to rest. I will make sure someone brings you something to eat later. While you are waiting for your memory to return, what should we call you?'

He cocked his head to one side. 'Call me Al.'

'Is that your name?'

He shrugged. 'Perhaps. It sounds right.'

She'd have to be satisfied with that for now. 'Very well. My name is Lady Johanne. I am mistress of Castle Brae.'

He smiled slightly and her heart stuttered again. 'Thank you for rescuing me, Lady Johanne, and for giving me your hospitality.'

She nodded and turned to go. As she did, she caught sight of his chest. She gasped and, without any rational thought, crossed the room to stand in front of him.

'I'm sorry. I wasn't thinking. I'd forgotten about the bruising and it looks so much worse today.' His chest was a myriad of purples and blues. 'No wonder you don't want to dress. You must be in agony. Here, let me help you.'

She turned to the mattress and grabbed his undershirt. She made towards him but before she reached him, he stepped backwards, holding out a hand to stop her, the skin of his cheeks a deep red. 'Please... I don't.'

'But...' The undershirt was soft in her hand. He inhaled deeply and let it out slowly.

'Thank you for your concern, Lady Johanne. You are right, I am in pain and bending to put clothes on will hurt, but I would very much like the dignity of dressing myself. I hope that you understand.'

Heat flooded Johanne's face. Of course a grown man wouldn't want help dressing, especially by a woman he barely knew. 'I… Yes. It was silly of me to suggest it. I have a son, you see. Sometimes, the mother in me takes over but you are obviously not a helpless child.' She waved a hand in the direction of his muscular body. 'I will leave you now.'

Without waiting for him to say anything else, she turned on her heel and tried to leave before remembering she still held his undershirt. She quickly strode to the bed and dumped the garment before leaving without saying another word.

Out in the corridor she sank slowly to her haunches, groaning in disbelief. What had possessed her to offer to dress the man? He wasn't a child. Not only that, he was also a stranger. He must think she was not right in the mind.

She forced herself upright. Now was not the time to second-guess herself. She must bury her embarrassment deep down and pretend she was not affected by what she had done. It did not matter what Al thought of her, so long as he was a good worker—that was all she needed.

Alewyn jerked awake. He'd been dreaming of flashes of lightning and the panicked scream of a horse. Had it been real? Was it a memory of what had happened to him or was it a nightmare, a hangover from the many battles he'd fought?

There was a soft sigh nearby, a sigh that didn't come from him and shouldn't be there. He bolted upright, muting a curse as his body screamed in agony. He was glad he had managed to restrain his yell when he caught sight of Lady Johanne poking at the fire in the grate. She knew he was injured; hell, she'd seen him with no clothes on and realised that he wasn't even able to dress himself properly, but he'd still prefer she think him strong.

As if she could hear him thinking about her, Johanne turned and caught sight of him watching her. Her welcoming smile caused his heart to thud uncomfortably.

'You're awake.'

'I am.'

'How is your...' She gestured to his body.

'Better, I think.' That was not entirely a lie. His muscles did not ache as much as they had. The damage could not be as bad as he had first feared.

'Good. I'm glad.' She placed the poker down. 'Has any memory of what happened to you returned?'

'I… Was there a storm before you found me?'

She nodded, stepping towards him. 'Yes. A violent one. Thunder and lightning and then endless rain. Do you remember it?' She sounded excited and not at all like a treacherous, conniving woman who was plotting the downfall of the country. Could a traitor be so…sweet? He supposed by their very nature a double-crosser would act differently depending on their audience and yet he couldn't help but feel she was being genuine. He could also think of no reason not to tell her the truth; there was nothing that revealed who he was or what he was doing in this part of the country.

'I was dreaming about flashes of light and the sound of my horse screaming in pain. I don't know if it is from a memory or not.'

She nodded again. 'There was rope across the path. Could your horse have run into it?

There was blood on the rope but none on you. If your horse ran into it at speed it would have been hurt. That would explain the screaming.'

He pushed his hair away from his face; he hated the thought of Ffleur damaged in any way and perhaps now lost without him. He closed his eyes; he could not think of that now. 'It is possible. If she did hit something unexpectedly, then I would have been thrown from my horse, which would explain some of the bruising, although perhaps not all.' He prodded his ribs. The pain was receding, thankfully, although he would want to leave it a few more days before getting in a fight.

'Do you have any enemies? Anyone who would want to see you hurt?' She moved away from him, making her way over to the window seat and sitting down in the alcove.

He swallowed. He did not like to lie but the situation demanded it. 'I am aware of no enemies.'

She nodded thoughtfully. 'I suppose if you have no memory, then you wouldn't know if you do or not.'

He didn't comment. He was quickly realising he did not enjoy feeding her mistruths. It was hard to tell if it was because her face was so open and trusting, so different to what he had been led to expect, or whether this overwhelming desire to be honest with her was a fundamental part of him. Perhaps he did not like living a lie. He had sworn an oath of honesty and integrity when he became a knight and lying went against that. He'd rather believe it was part of his personality and not because he was being drawn in by a pair of beautiful eyes.

'Do *you* have enemies?' He didn't expect her to answer; he was a stranger and there was no reason for her to trust him.

She pulled her knees up to her chest and whispered, 'Yes.'

His heart began to pound. She looked stricken. Surely, she was not about to confess to being an enemy of England. That would be too easy and yet what else could be causing such a guilty expression? He swallowed. 'Who is it?'

'Morcant.' Her eyes darted to the door as if expecting this enemy to burst through it.

He'd never heard the name before. 'Who?'

'Lord Morcant. He is my nearest neighbour. He…' She shuddered. 'Around here he is known for his cruelty. He wants to make me his wife but I do not want that. I…' She glanced at his chest and away again.

He looked down. He had managed to get his underclothes back on but he had left his outer shirt off. The pain of dressing had been too much. There was nothing for her to see, although she probably remembered well enough. 'You…?'

'I think he is the one behind your bruises,' she said in a rush. 'He may have known that I was travelling that path on the same day as you. The trap may have been for me or for Gemel. Actually, it was probably meant for Gemel.' As she spoke she stretched out her legs, looking less defeated and more like she was coming to a resolution. 'If Gemel were out of the way, Morcant probably believed I would be more willing to become his wife.'

Alewyn rubbed his temples as his head began to pound. 'Who's Gemel?'

'Gemel is my steward. Morcant doesn't believe I am ruling Brae by myself. I would imagine he thinks Gemel is the real power here. If Gemel were to die, then I would be a woman by myself. Morcant probably thinks I would welcome him then.' She snorted. 'I would rather die than be tied to another man, especially one such as him. He would be worse than Badon.' Colour swept across her cheeks as she seemed to realise how much she had said. She stood abruptly. 'You must be tired. I have kept you talking for ages. Here, I have brought you some food.' She strode over to the door and fetched a trencher that had been left beside it. 'I shan't ask if you want help with it. I doubt you will accept.'

He smiled as he took the food from her. 'Thank you, and yes, you are right. I would not like to be fed like a baby.'

She laughed. 'You are nothing like a baby.' Her cheeks coloured again. She turned away from him as if to hide her blush. 'I also brought you some clothes. The ones you were wearing when we found you were very fine. These ones will be better for working in, although they may be a little tight across the shoulders for there is no one as big as you at Brae.' She placed the clothes at the end of his mattress.

'Thank you for everything, Lady Johanne. I am deeply indebted to you.'

She nodded briskly. 'Well, I am sure you would do the same. I will bid you goodnight.'

She strode towards the door, stopping when

her hand rested on the handle. 'I would be grateful if you did not tell anyone of my fear.'

'What fear?'

'Of Morcant. I do not want my people to know how insistent he is becoming.'

'You have my word. I will tell no one of what we have spoken.'

'Thank you.' She let herself out, closing the door softly behind her. Alewyn stared at the space she had been. She was an odd character, Lady Johanne. One moment she was the tough, no-nonsense leader of a castle, the next she was soft and vulnerable. One thing she did not appear to be was treacherous. He'd been very keen to complete his mission, to prove himself to his family and his fellow knights, but now that he'd met her the thought of finding her guilty did not sit well with him at all.

The fire in the grate was down to its embers. Quietness was finally descending all around Brae. Cineas lay in the crook of her arm. Johanne leaned down and brushed her lips over the softness of his hair.

'Mama.'

'Yes, my love,' she whispered. She'd thought him nearly asleep and hoped this was not another request for a tale. Their time together was her favourite part of the day, but she was tired now and needed to rest herself before another long day tomorrow.

'Mary says there's a giant in the castle. Can I see him?'

'There's no giant, my love. There is a man here. He was injured and we are looking after him while he recovers.'

Cineas went quiet; Johanne hoped that was it. Sometimes Cineas's curiosity compelled him to ask many questions. It had been pointed out to her that the trait was not dissimilar to her own. She hoped she was a little more sophisticated than a six-year-old boy.

'Will he die?'

'No.'

'Then how is he hurt if he is so big?'

Johanne thought of the bruises that covered Al's broad chest. 'I think there was an accident.' She was not about to tell Cineas about Morcant. She still could not believe she had blurted all that out to Al. She never spoke to anyone about her fears, not even Gemel. Yet, there had been something so reassuringly calm about Al that had made her tell him things. She had not hidden her disgust at the thought

of marrying Morcant and had even implied
that marriage to Badon had been bad. Why?
It couldn't be because she thought Al handsome, although there was no denying that
she did. There was nothing special about that
though. There were plenty of attractive men
around, some of whom had made it clear they
would like to bed her. She had never been
even slightly tempted to share her body or her
thoughts.

'Can I see him?'

'When he is better. Now you must sleep.'

'Will you stay with me?'

'For a little longer.'

Cineas nodded sleepily against her arm. It
would not be long now before he was asleep
and then she could retire to her own chamber, the one place she was truly alone. The
one place she allowed herself some peace. If
Morcant got his wish, then he would want to
join her there.

'Mama, are you cold?'

'No, my love.'

'Then why are you shaking?'

'I... Perhaps I am a little cold. Try and rest
your eyes now.' Cineas seemed happy with her
answer, burrowing deeper beneath his covers.

She willed her body to calm down. There was no way she would bow down to pressure to marry Morcant, no matter what he threw at her. She would find a way to keep him out of her life and away from her sanctuary.

Chapter Three

A cold wind ripped through the courtyard. Alewyn tugged the edges of his cloak together and gazed about. Light and laughter spilled from a low building opposite him and the faint rush of the sea could be heard above the groan of the wind. He peered towards the castle's gate; no guards could be seen protecting the small stronghold and there was no movement on the ramparts above. No wonder Lady Johanne was so keen for him to stay; she was in desperate need of more manpower.

He stepped further into the courtyard. Gravel crunched beneath his feet and he paused. Should he use this opportunity to search the grounds? That's what his brother knights would do and so perhaps he should, although he wasn't really sure for what he was looking. He turned to step towards the keep when a small boy with coppery hair appeared out of the shadows, almost as if he had been lying in wait. 'Who are you? Are you the giant who has been healing his wounds at Brae?'

Alewyn cleared his throat. Children tended to avoid him because of his size, but this one was looking up at him with intense interest. 'I'm Al.'

The little boy nodded as if this explained everything. 'I'm the Baron of Brae but you can call me Cineas.'

'Good eve, Cineas.' Al had known Lady Johanne had a young son, the only child to survive from her marriage to the late baron. Seeing Cineas, so small and serious, made his heart twinge. If Alewyn found Lady Johanne guilty of her crimes, then this little boy would be motherless for she would undoubtedly hang.

'Are you going to the Great Hall to eat?'

'Yes.'

'My mother said you were not able to wake up when she found you. What does that feel like?'

'It felt like I was asleep.'

Cineas pulled a face, suggesting he was not

impressed by that answer. 'You're very big. Do you think I'll be as big as you one day?'

'Absolutely.'

Cineas grinned, pleased once more. 'Do you know how to use a sword?'

'Um.' Lying to a child was beyond the pale but what choice did he have? 'I'm having some trouble with my memory. Listen,' he cut in before the boy could continue with his questioning. 'Where can I find the Great Hall?'

Cineas pointed to the low building on the opposite side of the courtyard. 'Over there. You'd better hurry. They have already started eating.'

'Thank you. Are you going to come with me?'

'I've already had my food.' Cineas began walking in that direction anyway, trotting to keep up with Alewyn's long strides. 'Will you teach me how to use a sword?'

'Um…' He wasn't here to teach little boys sword skills but it could be a good way of gaining Lady Johanne's trust. As soon as he thought it, Alewyn's stomach twisted. Could he really do that? Use a child in this way. But then, what option did he really have? If Lady Johanne was guilty of what the King's Knights suspected, then she was a traitor to the Crown. Alewyn's mission was to use any means necessary to discover the truth.

The King's Knights had been aware for a while now of a plan to bring Frenchmen into England. Once in sufficient numbers, these men planned on gathering together and mounting an attack on King Edward within his own country, preventing a war on French soil. An informant had told them the men were coming into the country on Brae's coast. That had needed instant investigation.

'Well, could you?' prompted Cineas.

'If I can remember what to do, I'd be happy to teach you. With a wooden sword, of course.' He would do it but he wouldn't question Cineas about his mother. He drew a line there. 'Don't you have a trainer already living at Brae?'

'No. There are no squires here.'

Alewyn nodded to himself. It was no surprise. Squires would not want to train in a stronghold ruled by a woman. This was not a wealthy settlement. A quick glance around the courtyard had shown that Castle Brae needed urgent repair work. Lady Johanne needed funds; that was obvious even to the casual observer. Desperation could make people do all sorts of things they normally wouldn't and perhaps it had led Lady Johanne to treason. Time would tell.

At least now, Lady Johanne had unwittingly given Alewyn a reason to stay at Brae while he recovered his memory. This good fortune meant he could perform his investigation from within her walls. He would work with her men and win their trust. He would do whatever she asked him to do and gain her confidence. If there was anything to be found, he would discover it. His mission need not be a failure after all.

'There you are.' A young woman raced towards Cineas. 'You were supposed to wait for me.' The woman cast a horrified glance at Al. The type of look he was used to. People thought he was a brute, which was fine. It was helpful even. 'Come on,' continued the woman, tugging on Cineas's hand as if to try and get him away from a monster. 'It is long since time you were abed.'

Cineas gave a resigned sigh. 'Goodnight, Al.'

'Goodnight, Lord Cineas. Thank you for the pleasure of your company.' Alewyn's polite words did little to quell the suspicious glances of the young woman but Cineas grinned up at him before turning and walking back the way they had just come.

Alewyn continued towards the Great Hall, taking care to hide any pain in his gait. It would not do for anyone to see him limping; he wanted Lady Johanne to be aware of the strength of his body so that she quickly found a use for him. The sooner she began to depend on him, the better.

Lively chatter dimmed as he stepped into the hall. Families were grouped along the long wooden tables; they stopped eating and openly stared at him, but none of the interest felt hostile. At the far end, Lady Johanne sat at the high table, if you could call it that. There was none of the finery Alewyn was used to from his time at Windsor or his parents' stronghold, which almost resembled the King's in terms of opulence. Everything in this hall had seen better days and yet there was a warmth in the atmosphere here. A warmth he had not encountered before in a Great Hall and which made the muscles in his back relax even though he was in the strangest of situations.

Lady Johanne smiled at him as he approached and his heart lurched uncomfortably.

He was glad for the dim lighting in the room because he could feel his cheeks heating; he couldn't remember the last time his heart had been moved by the sight of a woman. Perhaps when he'd been a young squire but definitely not since he had entered adulthood. Lady Johanne gestured for him to join her. He made his way around the edge of the hall, aware of the curious gazes aimed his way.

Lady Johanne's smile deepened as he approached. He stumbled before righting himself. Her smile was like the sun coming out after a week of rain. He briefly stopped in his tracks, alarmed at his thought process. Now, he was practically spouting poetry. How humiliating. The blow to his head must have been more severe than he'd thought. He'd never thought about any woman in that way, never faltered when smiled at. Thank goodness no one knew what was in his mind. If she was a traitor, she could exploit his attraction, making him vulnerable. He would have to banish those thoughts. He could not afford to go around blushing and stumbling like a half-wit. Not now, when so much depended on him getting the next few days exactly right.

'I am pleased to see you are up and about,

Al. Please take a seat.' Lady Johanne indicated a chair to her left.

Alewyn lowered himself into it, clenching his jaw as his body protested vigorously to the movement. The urge to crawl back to the straw mattress was almost overwhelming. If he laid his head on the table, he was sure he would sleep. The smell of roast meat hit him and his stomach growled, his hunger taking over from his exhaustion. How long had it been since he'd last had a proper meal? His hopes that Lady Johanne hadn't heard his stomach were dashed when another smile crossed her face.

'I would imagine it takes a lot of food to keep a man the size of you fed.' She was smiling at him, her blue eyes full of amusement, and his heart stuttered. He frowned. What on God's earth was happening to him? It *must* be because of the blow to his head. His heart was acting like a young squire's with no connection to his mind. He needed to get it under his control. Until he proved otherwise, she was his enemy. He watched as her smile faded and the light in her eyes dimmed. 'That was insensitive of me. I'm sorry. You probably don't remember how much you normally eat.'

He experienced a twinge of guilt as she

turned away from him, her happiness dimmed by his lack of response. He pushed his remorse to one side. He was not here to make Lady Johanne feel good. He was here to prove to himself and those around him that his place in the King's Knights was justified. He was here to find out whether Lady Johanne was a traitor to the Crown and, if she was, it was his responsibility to ensure she was punished for such an awful crime. He could not afford to form any sort of attachment.

Lady Johanne turned to the person on her other side, an older, weathered man who glared at Alewyn from under bushy eyebrows.

Alewyn tore into the meat, pretending to focus all his attention on the food in front of him as he strained to hear what Lady Johanne was saying over the chatter in the hall. All he could make out was her concern about how the food stores were holding out in the face of the hard winter they were experiencing. There was no talk of France and the looming war with England but then she would hardly be so foolhardy as to talk about what she was purportedly doing in front of a stranger. He would have to be patient.

'Tomorrow we will need some stores shifting. Will you be strong enough?'

Alewyn started; he hadn't realised she'd turned to face him again. 'Aye, Lady Johanne. I want to be useful. Tell me what needs lifting, and I will do it for you.' Hopefully by tomorrow it wouldn't hurt so much to move. The sooner he could get on with helping her, the better. He had to hope she would ask him to help her with her less than legal activities, although he wouldn't rely on that happening. Being able to move freely around the castle would allow him to find out the truth some other way.

Lady Johanne picked up her goblet of wine and peered at him over the rim. 'Still no memories?'

'I'm sorry, my lady, but no.' His gut twisted at the lie, even though he knew the untruth was necessary.

'Gemel does not believe you. He thinks you are working with Morcant. Is that true?'

He admired her directness; he was so used to living among courtiers who did nothing but dissemble that her candour was refreshing. 'I can assure you that the first time I heard Lord Morcant's name was when you told me about him yesterday. I am not working for him.' He wondered if she would question that. If he really had lost his memory surely he wouldn't know if he was working for Morcant or not. He held his breath, waiting for Lady Johanne to point that out.

'Gemel said you would say something along those lines.' Lady Johanne nodded to the man on the other side of her. Gemel was still glaring at Alewyn but he said nothing, which Alewyn respected. Gemel let Johanne fight her own battles. Many men, regardless of their status, wouldn't be able to resist taking over.

He let out his breath; neither of them had questioned his denial. 'Your steward is right to be suspicious of me. I would be the same in his position. Perhaps you can explain why this Morcant wants to marry you and how my being employed by him would assist him, so I may reassure you I have had no dealings with the man.' He paused, his spoon halfway to his mouth. 'At least, I don't think I do; obviously I don't remember but perhaps if you talk about him, it will jolt my memory. I…' He stopped. He was talking too much; even he could see he was acting suspiciously. Why had he drawn attention to the fact that he couldn't remember anything moments after being pleased they hadn't noticed?

Johanne took a sip of her wine. Her tongue darted out to catch an errant drip and unwanted desire curled in Alewyn's stomach. He turned his gaze away. This wayward desire couldn't happen to him, not now. Not with this woman. Not when so much hung in the balance. He was losing his mind. First the ridiculous attraction and now, for the first time in his life, his mouth seemed to be running away from him.

Johanne did not appear to notice. 'As I mentioned yesterday, Morcant is one of my nearest neighbours. He has plans to make Brae his own because, although Brae is much smaller than his territory, acquiring the land will mean he has access to a large swathe of the coast. At the moment his plan is to coerce me into marriage, but I keep refusing and…' She paused and then appeared to decide something. 'And his patience is wearing thin. We believe he is behind a recent attempt on my life.'

Alewyn placed the joint he was holding back onto the trencher, his appetite suddenly gone. 'An attempt on your life. Do you mean what happened to me two days ago or something different?'

Johanne took another sip of wine. 'Something different. At least, I am sure an attempt was made on my life. I cannot prove it was Morcant but…' She shrugged. 'It was most likely him. He wants Brae. My son and I are in his way.'

'Are you sure he was behind the trap on the path?'

Lady Johanne shrugged. 'No, but… It was only a matter of time before he did something drastic. He will not care who or what gets hurt. He's…' A flash of something dark flitted across her eyes before she shook her head. 'It is not something you need to worry about.' She turned away from him then and began to talk to her steward once more.

Alewyn's head pounded. He wished one of his brother knights were with him, preferably Theo Grenville, who was a master at reading people's secrets in their body language and uncovering mysteries. He would have no problem working out whether Lady Johanne was a traitor or not and whether this Morcant was part of the problem or if this really was only a local territorial dispute.

But Theo had been sent to the north to deal with a different threat and Alewyn had vol-

unteered to come to Brae in his stead. Benedictus had tried to hide it, but Alewyn had
seen the scepticism on his brother's face after
his offer. Benedictus's look had suggested he
didn't think Alewyn was up to the challenge
of this mission. That moment had solidified
everything for Alewyn. He swore to himself
that he would find out what was happening
and finally make his brother and the rest of
his family proud of him.

He clenched his jaw to stop himself from
groaning out loud.

All this speculation and thinking was too
much when his body hurt so. He had to hold
himself upright to avoid slumping in the chair.
Weariness tugged at his limbs. There was so
much to ponder and whatever happened to him
before Lady Johanne had found him unconscious had stolen his energy. Even if he wasn't
covered in bruises, he wasn't sure he was up
to the task anyway. Give him some enemies to
pummel and he was the right man for it but this
level of subtlety was beyond him. He wanted
nothing more than to crawl back to the straw
mattress and sleep for several more days or to
make his way back to Windsor and admit he

didn't know how to proceed. But that wasn't an option. England's safety was resting on him.

He picked up his joint again; he would do whatever it took to find out the truth.

The doors to the Great Hall banged open. Alewyn reached for his sword, cursing when he realised it wasn't by his side.

All chatter ceased.

A stocky man stood, framed by the doorway.

Lady Johanne put her goblet down and slowly got to her feet. If Alewyn hadn't been so close to her he wouldn't have noticed her trembling fingers, but she stood tall and proud, as if men barging into her space did not daunt her.

'Lord Morcant,' she said calmly and everything in Alewyn froze. Here was the man who caused Lady Johanne to shudder with revulsion. If he hadn't seen her do that only yesterday, then he would never have been able to tell from her stance and her words. 'How good of you to join us. I'm afraid you are too late to join our celebratory feast but I will still accept your congratulations.' Now what was she talking about? What celebrations?

The short, thickset man strode down the centre of the room as if it was his own Great

Hall. Alewyn's fists clenched at his audacity. If Lady Johanne wanted, Alewyn would crush this man like the flea he was, no matter the bruising on his own body or the fact that she might be a traitor.

Morcant kept coming and Alewyn forced himself to remain completely still when every fibre of his being wanted to jump up and drag the man away from this scene. Nobody moved to stop him but Alewyn noticed many of the women dropping their gaze to the food in front of them. This man was not welcome here and not just by Lady Johanne.

'My congratulations? I do not understand.' Morcant sounded amused, as if Lady Johanne had told a whimsical joke.

Lady Johanne appeared to ignore the patronising tone because she replied happily, 'Oh, I thought you must have heard the news and come racing to see me, hence your interruption of our feast. But it's of no matter. Please allow me to introduce my betrothed.' She swept her hand towards Alewyn.

Alewyn blinked. What?

The other man stopped in his stride. 'Your betrothed?' Morcant sounded as shocked as Alewyn.

Alewyn held himself still, willing himself not to show any reaction. Until he knew what game was being played here, he would go along with this charade.

'Yes, my betrothed.' Johanne sounded supremely confident, as if her statement was nothing other than the complete truth.

Alewyn glanced at Gemel; if anything his fists were even tighter than Alewyn's, suggesting that he knew nothing of this development. What game was Lady Johanne playing and, most importantly, how could Alewyn use it to his advantage?

Chapter Four

Sweat dripped down Johanne's spine as the silence stretched on, the hall a tableau of frozen faces. Her fingers shook. She'd risked everything to keep Brae out of Morcant's control, but this was her biggest throw of the dice to date. This was where everything she had carefully constructed over the last four years, all the control she had won, could fall down. This was where she could lose her son's inheritance and in front of all those whose livelihoods depended on her.

She had wagered everything on Al, a man she barely knew and whom Gemel, quite rightly, didn't completely trust. Al could easily be in Morcant's employ and she could have made a spectacular fool of herself. Although that was nothing if she had destroyed the very legacy she was trying to save.

She sensed Al standing up beside her. Lying down, he had been formidable. The way the horse had staggered under his weight had given some indication of his size but she still hadn't really appreciated how big he was. She was a tall woman but he towered over her, and the breadth of him… He could easily crush her and everyone in the hall if he so wished.

She held her breath as she waited for the moment to unfold.

'Please, Lord Morcant, take a seat at our table, so you may join in with our celebrations.' Al's voice rumbled through her and Johanne's knees began to shake uncontrollably as relief swept through her. If she'd been able, she would have flung her arms around Al. Instead, she held herself still.

Morcant stood before them, not moving, his gaze flicking between Al and her. Morcant was not a subtle man. If he knew Al it would show on his face. The hostile glare he sent Al suggested he had never seen him before. 'I have heard nothing of this. When did your betrothal occur?'

Johanne jumped as Al growled, the noise

deep and threatening. 'Show my lady some respect in her own home or I'll throw you out. I do not care if you are to be my new neighbour or not.'

Morcant's jaw hung slack.

The hall was silent, even the children had stopped chattering; it was as if everyone was holding their breath as they waited to see what would happen. Nobody spoke to Morcant like that and lived to tell the tale.

On Morcant's infrequent visits, Johanne placated him, keeping his infamous temper at bay by distracting him. She had learned the skills during her volatile marriage and having to employ them again made her stomach churn. Tonight, greeting Morcant brightly had been an effort of will, but she did it because she'd lived with the consequences of defying a violent man and it was not something she wanted to experience again.

She had never seen anyone defy Morcant in such an open display of strength. Even Badon had humoured him to a certain extent. Beside her, Gemel's hand moved slowly towards his sword. Johanne knew that Al had no weapon on him but she didn't doubt he would be able to defend himself if Morcant turned violent. Even without the two men side by side, it was obvious who was the taller and stronger of the two.

The moment seemed to stretch for an eternity until Morcant blinked at Al, looking so much like a startled owl Johanne had to bite her lips to stop a gurgle of laughter. Eventually, Morcant bowed his head slightly. 'I apologise for my tone, Lady Johanne, I was merely surprised. I would be honoured to join you in your celebrations.'

Morcant took a seat nearby and Johanne sank gratefully back onto her chair. Al was slower to move. He kept his gaze focused on Morcant; only when he seemed sure the other man was not going to pose an immediate threat did he seat himself, the chair creaking under his bulk.

The members of her household began to eat again but there was no lively chatter and the normal jovial atmosphere was dimmed. It reminded Johanne of meals taken when her husband was alive. Meals that were mostly silent save for his booming voice. If Badon was in a good mood, he would be full of praise for himself. If, as was often the case, something had happened to cause him to lose his temper he would growl and snap at anyone unlucky enough to be caught in his gaze.

Johanne placed her hands in her lap; her appetite completely vanished as old feelings of inadequacy washed over her. To her surprise, Al reached over and took her hands in one of his, his skin warm and dry around hers. He squeezed gently and then let go. She was pathetically grateful for the reassuring gesture. It had been a long time since anyone had realised she might need one.

When she was sure her hands were no longer shaking, she picked up her goblet and had a long sip of wine. The warmth of the fruity drink ran through her, giving her the strength to carry on, and if her voice sounded strained, only those who knew her well would notice. 'If you did not come to wish us happiness, why are you here, Morcant?'

Morcant wiped his mouth on his sleeve. 'I came to check on you, Lady Johanne. The troubles with France are rising and living on the coast is dangerous for a woman alone. I am worried for you as a concerned neighbour.'

Anger spiked through her and she welcomed its return. Fury gave her power. 'I am not alone, as I have pointed out many times to you.'

'Indeed,' growled Al. 'And now she has me, your presence is no longer needed.'

Morcant's lips pursed. 'And who are you exactly?'

Johanne squirmed in her chair. She should have anticipated this since the moment Al had extended his invitation to Morcant to stay. Al shifted in his seat, the movement only perceptible to Johanne. Her fingers tightened on her goblet and she forced them to relax. It would do no good if she threw it across the room.

'I am Sir Alewyn,' said Al.

'And who are your people, Sir Alewyn?'

Johanne leaned forward. 'I'm not sure I like your tone of questioning, Morcant.' She could hardly expect Al to lie any more on her behalf. To create a family with no warning was not fair to him.

Morcant turned his rigid gaze to her. 'I apologise again, Lady Johanne. You must know that I am merely looking after your interests. I…'

How dare he! 'If my noble brother says Sir Alewyn is good enough for me, then who am I to argue.'

Morcant's gaze flickered between them again. Al remained silent, a formidable statue by her side.

'So, this is an arranged betrothal.'

'Of course.'

'And yet your brother is not here to witness the celebrations.'

Alewyn stood. 'I am sure you do not mean to insult my betrothed with your many impertinent questions but I am afraid you have outstayed your welcome. Allow me to escort you back to your horse.'

Morcant's mouth hung open once again as the hall descended into silence. Talking back to Morcant was one thing, throwing him out was quite another. Johanne didn't know of anyone who had ever had the audacity to do it. She had only been able to withstand Morcant for so long because he had hoped to form a marriage alliance with her. Now that path was cut off to him, Johanne had no idea how he would react, especially with this blatant hostility from Al. Things could go terribly wrong. Or perhaps this was what Brae needed, perhaps a show of strength would get him to back away and finally leave her and her people alone.

Morcant didn't rise from his seat. Johanne

wiped her hands on her dress. She didn't want violence to break out in her hall, not with all the innocent families dining. Al continued to stare at Morcant, hostility coming off him in waves. He muttered something she didn't catch and then began to move around the table. Her heart quickened, but whether that was from fear or from some other emotion, she wasn't sure. Al reached Morcant and towered over him. Al's size made Morcant appear almost childlike. For a long moment the two men stared at each other; Johanne barely dared to breathe. Finally, Morcant rose and stalked out of the hall. Al glanced back at Johanne, nodded once and then strode out after him.

'Gemel, follow them and see what is said.'

Gemel glared at her. 'Aye, mistress, and then we will talk.'

Johanne didn't nod in return. Her heart was racing uncontrollably. Although she'd sent Gemel out to check what was said between Al and Morcant, she couldn't deny that part of her was worried for Al's safety, which was ridiculous for several reasons. Al was clearly a man who could look after himself, but she had seen his slight limp as he walked into the hall and the way he'd grimaced as he sat down.

She did not want to be responsible for making him worse. That was the cause of this concern. It wasn't that she cared about him specifically. They had only just met and not had more than two conversations. She batted away the memory of him sleeping, the way he had looked so vulnerable despite his size. He was not defenceless; he could take care of himself.

She should worry about herself instead. Gemel would want to know what her plan was and she was loath to admit that she didn't have one. She may have given herself a temporary reprieve with this false betrothal but it may make things harder in the future. But she did not owe her steward an explanation. This was her stronghold. The decisions she made, whether they were right or wrong, were hers to make. She had fought for too long and too hard to give away that authority to anyone and Gemel had no right to second-guess her.

This evening, seeing Morcant striding into Brae's Great Hall as if he was the lord and master of the place, as if he was already her husband and could act how he wished, had snapped something inside her. She'd wanted him gone from her life and, for one blinding moment, she thought she'd found a solution. Blurting out that she was going to marry Al was not her finest moment. She doubted Gemel was right about Al collaborating with Morcant in some way. Morcant had not shown any recognition of the man, but if she were wrong, then she had just played straight into their hands.

She didn't know why and, even though it was ridiculous, even though there was no reason behind it and she could be being the biggest fool who had ever lived, she trusted Al not to be in league with Morcant. Despite his intimidating bulk, his eyes were thoughtful and kind. He did not seem to fall into the same category of men like Badon and Morcant.

Her mother would curse her for being a gullible fool, for being led by her eyes rather than her intelligence. It was true that Al was a fine-looking man, with his broad shoulders and dark eyes, and as a woman who had never known what it was like to have a good lover, his muscled arms appealed to her. He looked as if he'd know what to do with a woman in his bed; perhaps it would be a pleasant experience rather than a chore that must be endured.

She sighed; she would never know. She was not going to take Al as a lover while he was staying at Brae. Even if she could get over her repulsion for the act, she could not risk a pregnancy—another mouth to feed would be disastrous. She shook her head; she had no idea why she was thinking of this now. She should be working out how to manage the outcome of this evening and not thinking of Al's body.

Johanne had only managed a few sips of her wine before Morcant's arrival, perhaps that's why she was entertaining such ridiculous thoughts. Gemel's insistence, before Al joined them, that Al may not be trustworthy had shaken her more than she'd wanted her steward to know. She'd tried to appear unconcerned but she wasn't convinced she'd managed to hide her trembling fingers from either of them. Now her gut was churning and the thought of eating caused bile to rise in her throat but she had to eat. She had to carry on with the charade of appearing calm and in control; whatever she did next would dictate how the rest of her household reacted to Morcant's appearance and her own wild announcement.

She picked up her spoon and compelled herself to swallow some of the stew. As she forced the food into her mouth, not tasting a single bite, the chatter of the hall began to rise. By the time Al and Gemel stepped back inside, it was almost as if nothing had happened.

She carried on eating as the men approached, giving every impression she was relaxed. She'd learned early on in her marriage that if she showed even the slightest emotion, Badon would manipulate it for his own ends and, over the years, she had got good at pretending nothing bothered her.

'You can trust him,' was all Gemel said as he slipped back into his chair and began to eat once again.

Al did not sit. 'I'd like a word in private if you please, Lady Johanne.'

She nodded once but didn't stand until she had finished every last drop of stew in her bowl. She was the one in control and he needed to remember that. Once she'd forced down the last mouthful, she carefully placed her spoon back down. 'We'll talk in my antechamber. I will not conduct my private affairs in front of everyone.'

She walked out, back straight, not waiting to see if he would follow her. After a moment, she heard his heavy footsteps behind her. They didn't speak until he had closed the door behind him.

For a beat they stood, staring at each other. Her pulse began to beat wildly in her throat but she kept her hands loosely at her side.

'What on God's earth just happened?' Al pushed his dark hair away from his eyes. 'I find myself betrothed to a woman with no warning that something so...' He began to pace; words seemed beyond him.

Her instinct was to apologise for putting him in a difficult position but she held her tongue. She would not show him just how close to the edge she was or how much she needed him to go along with the fake betrothal. She did not want his pity. 'As I explained earlier, Morcant has been pestering me to marry him for some time. He's a violent man whom I wouldn't want to marry even if he was in love with me. As it is, he wants to add Brae to his land and he can't understand why I keep saying no to his frequent proposals of marriage. He's getting increasingly frustrated and, after the recent attack on my life, my fear is that he will turn his violence towards my son. Tonight, I finally found a way to put a stop to his demands.'

Al shook his head as he prowled around the edges of the chamber, dominating the small space. 'And when we don't marry? Won't you be back in your original position, only weakened without the protection of my name?'

When she'd been forcing her stew down, Johanne had thought about this. 'He's not to know that we're not married. I will put it about that the marriage happened. Once you leave, I will say that you have gone to France to join the war, or if there is no war, I will say you have gone abroad to train.' She waved her hand around. 'I will figure out the details later. This could buy me a couple of years. I only need to hold on to control until my son is a little older, then he will take over the running of Brae and marriage to me will not mean that Morcant gains a territory. This pretend betrothal gives me time to prepare for the future. It is not as if I am really asking you to marry me and so there really is no difficulty for you.'

Al stopped in the centre of the room. 'I don't think this is a good idea. Any one of your serfs could talk to Morcant and tell him the truth. It is a foolish falsehood.'

How dare he call her foolish! Impetuous maybe, thoughtless perhaps, but not foolish. She would do anything to protect Brae. 'But it is already done. And I don't believe any of my people would talk to Morcant. He is universally disliked.'

Al began pacing in the opposite direction. Guilt as well as irritation began to edge in on Johanne. She hadn't meant to make him feel uncomfortable, but really, he was making it into something it wasn't. 'I truly expect nothing from you. You mustn't think I want to marry you any more than you want to marry me. I will never wed another man, never be subjected to the whims of someone else. This is purely a delaying tactic on my behalf. Morcant is unlikely to visit again while you are with me and so we can carry on as we planned.'

Al stopped and shook his head. 'No. That won't work. Your people will need to see me as your betrothed. For your plan to succeed, there can be no doubt in anyone's minds that we are going to wed.'

'Don't be ridiculous. No—'

'Lady Johanne, I am not being ridiculous. To make this plan work, we would need to present a united front. Everyone needs to believe we intend to marry. Even those closest to you. What if I regain my memory tomorrow and realise I have somewhere urgent I need to be? What then?'

Johanne clasped her hands in front of her. She needed Al to go along with her plan, she needed it far more than she would ever confess, but…she wasn't going to force him because that went against everything she believed in. She knew what it was like to have someone dominate your will, to have your life and joy sucked from you as you mindlessly did the bidding of someone else. Badon had controlled her every moment and, at his death, she had sworn not to treat anyone in that way while she was leader of Brae. There was a fine line between being a leader and a controller of lives and she did not want to cross it.

Despair threatened. She would not force Al and she did not know how to make him do what she wanted. She thought that she had found a solution. One that would give her son the security he needed. She hadn't, for one moment, thought that Al would not go along with her plan. He needed her. He had nowhere else to go and surely being betrothed to her was not such an awful thing.

Al was watching her; she turned her face away, not wanting him to witness her distress.

'Lady Johanne, I know I owe you a huge debt of gratitude. If you had not found me, there is no doubt I would have died. I did not mean for my words to upset you.'

'I am not upset.' Her words came out croaky and heat swept across her cheeks. She sounded on the verge of tears and she never showed that sort of weakness to anyone, not any more.

She heard his soft groan and then he took a step towards her. 'Please don't cry.'

'I'm not,' she snapped. She needed him to stop being compassionate. It was making it harder to retain her authoritative stance. She was so unused to kindness it was causing her undoing.

'Perhaps we can make your plan work.' His voice rumbled behind her. 'I could stay for a while and act as if we are planning a wedding...'

Her heart leapt; she turned to him. 'You would do that?'

'Yes.'

She turned and found he had stepped nearer to her. This close she realised his eyes weren't as dark as she'd first thought. They were a rich, dark brown, like freshly polished wood, and full of compassion. 'Thank you. We'll tell my people you were on your way here when you had an accident. There's been speculation about who you are but neither Gemel nor I have said anything that will contradict that idea. You won't regret this. And I'm sorry about blurting it out the way I did. I didn't mean to make you feel uncomfortable.'

He wiped her tears away, the tips of his fingers brushing lightly against her skin. 'I know. I understand that you wanted to protect your son. I am sorry I reacted so badly. You are right. It is nothing for me to pretend that we are betrothed while I stay here. If it helps to keep Morcant away, then that is a small price to pay for your hospitality.'

She smiled and the answering warmth in his eyes sent a delicious shiver running down her spine. He must have felt it too because his gaze dropped to her lips and her stomach lurched. Did he want to kiss her? She couldn't allow that. He was staying with her because he had nowhere else to go, not because there was going to be a real betrothal between them.

She stepped backwards out of his grip, relieved when he let her go easily. 'It won't be a real betrothal.'

'I know.'

'There won't be any kissing.'

Colour spread across his cheeks and any warmth in his eyes vanished. 'I know that too, my lady.'

She nodded. Good. That was what she wanted. And the odd twinge of disappointment she felt in her breast at his agreement was utter nonsense. She didn't *want* to kiss him. Despite being married, she had never been kissed. Badon hadn't seen the point and, until this moment, she had never missed it. Not that she wanted to be kissed now, it was just his lips looked so…

'If you will excuse me, Lady Johanne, I would like to return to my chamber.' The friendliness had dropped from his voice. 'Tomorrow will be a long day and I fear my body needs more rest to recover from my injuries.'

'Of course. Thank you for your aid this evening.'

It was strange to be so formal after they had held one another but it was for the best. If she were to survive the coming months, then she must do so without thinking of touching the man she was using to help her keep hold of Brae.

Chapter Five

Alewyn swung the axe and brought it down on the wood he was chopping. It split with a satisfying thwack. He placed another log on the support and wiped sweat away from his eyes. He welcomed the physical work; it was a good distraction from the utter failure of his mission so far. Three days in and he was making no progress. It was as frustrating as hell.

'The wood never stood a chance against you, did it?' Edmund, the castle's carpenter, was watching Alewyn at work. He was friendly and supportive but not at all informative. If there was a plot to undermine the King, Edmund was not part of it and knew nothing of it. In such a small community, was it possible to commit a crime on the scale necessary to bring a legion of Frenchmen into the country without everyone having an inkling that something was going on? Or was he just hoping that was the case because he didn't want Johanne to be guilty because deep down he wanted to bed her and that was a huge conflict of interest.

Alewyn wiped the sweat off his brow. 'Cutting through those logs was like slicing through air. Don't you have anything more challenging for me to do?'

Edmund laughed. He seemed to get great joy out of Alewyn's strength, always trying, and failing, to find something Alewyn couldn't physically do.

'How long can you keep this up?'

'All day if needs be.' That was not true. His muscles still ached from whatever had happened to him before Lady Johanne found him; he would like to stop soon but he wouldn't. He'd keep going for however long was necessary to gain people's trust. 'How much more have we got to go?'

'All that lot.' Edmund gestured to a pile of wood behind them. Edmund was clutching his own axe but he hadn't chopped any wood in quite some time. Alewyn wasn't going to point that out. If he could make a friend here, someone who would confide in him, perhaps that friend would introduce him to someone who did know something and he could make some progress on the damned mission.

'Your lady will be pleased with our morning's work.' Edmund waggled his eyebrows; Alewyn laughed.

Lady Johanne had not told any of her people that their betrothal was a pretence, which Alewyn was pleased about. She'd seemed so sure none of her people would betray her, but that was naive. If there was a spy amongst their ranks, then Morcant would know Lady Johanne had lied to him, so Alewyn was glad she had listened to his insistence they make their betrothal look real. But it was causing other problems. Because her people believed it, he was being treated with a respect he had yet to truly earn.

Realising he had not responded to Edmund, Alewyn mumbled, 'I hope so. I want to please Lady Johanne.'

'Aye, she's a rare woman, generous and principled.'

Alewyn let out a long breath. The difficulty with all this respect for Lady Johanne was that no one would talk about her in any detail. They evaded his questions about the baroness and her steward and only ever spoke of her with high praise. He'd frequently heard that she was a kind and fair leader, a leader who never shirked her duties and worked as hard as anyone else, if not more so. He'd learned that she was devoted to her son but that she never indulged him. Even at only six years of age, Cineas was being taught how to behave as a nobleman. That was the sum of all he had learned.

'When's the wedding?' Alewyn jumped. He had forgotten Edmund was there.

'The wedding is…' Alewyn trailed off, not knowing what to say.

'You're leaving it to her to decide,' Edmund supplied for him. 'Can't say I blame you. Life is easier when women think they are having their own way of things.' He laughed at his own joke. 'Mind you, I'm sure you'll want to hurry up and get it done. Anyone can see you're smitten.'

Edmund laughed again as heat rushed across Alewyn's face. He bent back to the logs to hide his reaction to the gentle teasing. He wasn't smitten. Yes, he was watching her. He was in Brae to keep an eye on her doings. If he enjoyed looking at her whenever she passed by, that was natural. She was a beautiful woman; any man would react in the same way. It didn't mean anything more than that. Fortunately, Edmund did not press Alewyn further because he really didn't want to dwell on how often his eyes strayed towards Johanne in a way that had nothing to do with his mission and had everything to do with her willowy grace.

Alewyn carried on splitting logs, losing himself in the rhythm. Edmund wandered away at some point. When Alewyn heard the man's distant laugh, he paused, turning the axe blade-side down and resting against the handle.

Far up on the battlements he caught a glimpse of coppery hair. He held his breath, hoping to be rewarded with a sight of her. Shortly she came into view, bending slightly and holding her braids away from her face. She was addressing someone smaller than her, and from the smile that spread across her face, Alewyn knew she must be talking to Cineas. The love in her eyes when she looked at the little boy caused a slight pang in Alewyn's chest. No one had ever looked at him like that.

He glanced down at his pile of logs. He was nearly done for today. When he was finished, he would make sure he spoke to Lady Johanne.

He'd been hoping that the fake betrothal would allow him more time with her. More time to figure whether she was a clever mastermind working to bring down England from within or whether she was an innocent. But he'd been wrong, and after three long days of working on menial tasks around the castle he was no closer to her or to discovering even the tiniest of details.

Any attempts to talk to Lady Johanne in depth were thwarted. During mealtimes, she kept up a lively conversation, chatting away to her steward or anyone else on the table. As her betrothed, he continued to sit to her left; she'd converse with him about his day but she skilfully cut off talk of anything deeper. She was so good at it that, at first, he hadn't realised it was happening. It was only during last night's repast he had noticed her clever deflection.

If he wasn't investigating her, he would be thoroughly charmed by the laughter that lurked in the depths of her eyes. As it was, he was having a hard time thinking of anything other than the image of placing his hand on the curve of her hip. He wanted to see whether his hand did fit there as perfectly as he imagined. He wanted to make her laugh, to see the slant of her mouth directed solely at him. He'd spent more time than he'd care to admit imagining the things he could say to make that happen.

It was not good. It was not why he was here. And if by some miracle she proved innocent of being a traitor and wasn't totally against having another husband, she was not a suitable wife for him. He'd need a wife who would be there as a support for him, someone who would make life easy at the end of a long, hard campaign, someone gentle. A woman whose main priority was a small stronghold on the south coast of England was not right for him.

The handle of his axe bit into his arm. He picked it back up and began to chop the last of the logs, the split giving him some satisfaction from his building frustration. He shouldn't even be thinking about Lady Johanne in any other capacity than as a suspect. There had never been a more critical moment to uphold his solemn oath to serve the King, forsaking all personal feelings. England was on the verge of war with France. No matter what he felt about the reasons behind the conflict, the work he did now was crucial in the effort to make sure that England was the victor.

He could not fail.

And he had to complete his mission quickly.

Benedictus would expect results and he would expect them soon. Alewyn didn't know how long he had been on the mission when Lady Johanne found him on the path. He didn't think it had been long. He remembered riding from Windsor. The weather had been awful, cold with ice pellets hitting his face as they rained down from the sky. His thoughts had all been on getting to Brae as quickly as possible; he'd had no plans for a detour. Every time he tried to recall what had happened, his memories slipped through his fingers like ghosts.

A quick calculation had him guessing that if he didn't return to Windsor within fourteen days, then Benedictus would send someone to find him and get a report. It would be beyond humiliating if all he had done by this time was a few small repairs on the walls of Castle Brae and chopped some logs for firewood. It would probably cost him his place in the King's Knights. If it didn't, it would be down to his brother, and Alewyn didn't think he could live with himself if that were the case.

He swung his axe again. The wood splintered and he set it to one side. Whatever else happened today, he must speak with Lady Johanne before the sun set.

'What are you doing?'

Alewyn dropped his axe and it clattered to the ground. He'd been so absorbed in his thoughts he hadn't heard anyone approach. Some spy he was. He straightened to find Cineas watching him.

'I'm chopping wood.' Surprise at being caught unawares made him stupid. He half expected the young baron to turn away in disgust. It was obvious what Alewyn was doing. But to his surprise the boy stayed exactly where he was.

'Can I have a go?'

Alewyn glanced down at the long, sharp blade; he couldn't imagine it in the hands of someone so small. 'I'm not sure that's a good idea. Your mother would have my head if you got hurt.'

The blue eyes squinted. 'What would she do with it?'

Alewyn frowned. 'Do with what?'

'Your head?'

Alewyn laughed. 'I meant that she would kill me if you were injured because I was so foolish as to give you such a sharp blade.'

The boy looked him up and down, pausing over the breadth of his shoulders. It was a look Alewyn had seen many a time. 'There's no way my mother could kill you. You're too big.'

'Aye. That's probably true.'

'So, I can have a go then.' The young lad held out his hand.

'Cineas, leave Al alone.'

Alewyn's heart jolted uncomfortably as he looked up to see Lady Johanne standing nearby. He turned his gaze back to the chopped logs; he was meant to be investigating her, not being struck dumb by her beauty. He was a big, lumbering idiot.

'Cineas, run on inside for me. I need to talk to Al.'

'But, Mama, Al was going to let me have a go of his axe.'

Alewyn blinked as a deep frown settled across Lady Johanne's brow. Why had the lad said that? He hadn't been about to do anything of the sort. Surely, she wouldn't think he would allow anyone so small near something so dangerous. 'No, I—'

Lady Johanne wasn't glaring at him, but at her young son. 'Don't lie, Cineas. I heard Al tell you he was not going to let you anywhere near a sharp blade. I will see you inside. Go ahead, please.'

The boy's whole body sagged but he did as he was told, trudging indoors without any further complaint. Johanne shook her head. 'He's so dramatic. It's amusing but I do wish he wouldn't lie to me.'

'I doubt he saw it as a lie. My objection was that you would kill me if I allowed him anywhere near the blade. Once he'd established that you would be unlikely to physically overcome me, he thought the argument won.'

Lady Johanne laughed, her blue eyes sparkling, and Alewyn's heart warmed. 'He will need to be near sharp blades soon, I would have thought. It cannot be long before he begins his knight's training.'

Her smiled ebbed away. 'It's a year away. There will be time enough.'

Alewyn had been taught to hold a sword almost as soon as he could stand. His parents had never protected him from the brutality of life; it had been quite the opposite. His parents had believed Benedictus and he should show no fear when it came to fighting. Alewyn knew nothing about raising children and he was not about to criticise Lady Johanne, not when there were more important things to be done. 'You wanted to speak to me, my lady.'

'I did. Tonight, Baron Yonescu is going to dine with me… I mean, us. He is one of my neighbouring barons. He is loosely supportive of me and has, on occasion, promised to send aid should Morcant become more threatening with his demands. I value his support greatly. He has sent a message that he wishes to visit in order to congratulate us on our betrothal, so you will need to wear your finer clothes.'

Could this be the opportunity Alewyn had been waiting for? Surely, he could use this to discover more about her. 'Will we dine in private or in the Great Hall?'

'In private. Yonescu prefers it. Gemel is normally with me but tonight it should be you instead.'

Alewyn nodded slowly. He could work this to his advantage. He had to. 'Then you and I should talk before he arrives.'

She frowned. 'What about?'

'I know nothing about you.'

'We would hardly be the first couple to enter a marriage knowing nothing but our first names. I don't think there is anything of importance you need to know.'

'It is true that couples often know nothing of each other. But you told Morcant that our betrothal was arranged through your brother. As I've no idea where he lives or who he is or anything about him at all, the lie will unravel quickly if I am questioned about his or your life.'

He held his breath as Lady Johanne considered his words. 'Very well. Once you have finished with the wood, come and find me in my antechamber. It is the room we spoke in before, behind the Great Hall. We will talk.'

He nodded once before bending back to the wood, shielding his expression from her. It would not do for her to realise how pleased he was with this development. His heart felt lighter than it had in days. All he had to do later was turn their conversation to France; how hard could that be? Everyone was talking about France these days; it would be the most natural thing in the world to bring the troubles with the country into the conversation. Finally, he could begin to make some progress. He grinned as his axe severed another log. It was the prospect of progress that was making him so happy; it was nothing to do with the fact he was going to be spending time alone with Lady Johanne.

He returned to his bedchamber before he went to Lady Johanne's private chambers. After a morning chopping wood, he could smell himself. His nose wrinkled in disgust as he stripped himself of the clothes he had been lent to work in and washed away the sweat. The bruising on his chest was finally beginning to fade. He was mostly able to move without pain and in a few days it would be as if nothing had happened to him.

He went to pull on his own clothes but decided he had best keep them clean for the meal with Yonescu as Lady Johanne had requested them specifically. He was still trying to stay in her good graces. Reluctantly, he pulled on his borrowed clothes once more. He would have to work out the best place to clean them because he did not want to stink. He ran his fingers through his hair before stopping, his fingers still in the strands, as realisation washed over him. He was trying to make himself look good before he went to see Lady Johanne. And he had to be honest with himself. It was not because he thought that if he looked good she was more likely to tell him what he wanted to know. It was because he wanted her to look at him the way he knew he looked at her.

He deliberately ruffled his hair, messing it up. Yes, when she smiled at him, he lost control of his thoughts, but he could stop that. All he had to do was focus. It was only a matter of training himself not to react to her and he could do that. One thing he did excel at was training.

Lady Johanne was already in her antechamber, sitting at a desk and filling in columns in a large ledger.

She glanced up as he stepped into the room. His heart jolted as their eyes met. It seemed his talk to himself had done no good; his body still reacted to her. He hadn't mastered his sword in a day. There was still hope he could get this unwanted attraction quickly under control and, if he couldn't, there was no need for her to know about it.

Turning away from her, he moved over to the fireplace and watched the flames flickering over the wood. 'Thank you for agreeing to meet with me.'

Lady Johanne cleared her throat. 'I should be thanking you. You are doing me a great personal favour. I am sorry if I have not appeared more grateful before today. I am not used to relying on people for aid and, well…' Her voice faded away. He glanced back to look at her. She shook her head and squared her shoulders. He turned back to the fire. It was easier to concentrate if he wasn't looking directly at her. 'What is it you would like to know about my brother and I?' she asked.

'I…' He'd only thought about this conversation in terms of how he could find out about France, not about her brother, but he could hardly leap into her relations with the French straight away. 'How old are you?' he asked instead.

He heard the rustle of her skirts but he managed to refrain from turning around. 'I don't think Yonescu will ask you my age, but I passed my twenty-fourth summer this year.'

Quite a bit younger than his thirty years then. Not that it mattered. 'Who makes up your family?'

'My parents are dead. I have a sister in St Helena's nunnery and another married to a nobleman in the North. I haven't seen either of them in years. My brother is Baron Torquil. His stronghold is two days northwest of here in Tenterden and that was where I lived until I married.'

A log fell in the grate and the fire hissed. Alewyn picked up a poker and prodded the embers, sending sparks flying. He had heard of Baron Torquil but Lady Johanne's brother was not a man who frequented Windsor. Alewyn couldn't put a face to the name. 'Is Baron Torquil the type to marry you off to a man you don't know?'

'My brother is very self-interested and does not really care what I do. However, I am sure that if a union between you and I benefitted him in some way, then yes, I would think that he would push for the match.'

'Then why don't we say that...' Alewyn shrugged. He could not think of a single reason why their marriage would benefit anyone other than himself. A fleeting image of Lady Johanne, her curls spread across his bed, crossed his mind. His body tightened and he was glad she could not see his face; if she looked at him now, she would know exactly what he thought of her.

'How about this?' Johanne supplied. 'You met me when I visited my brother during the summer. You were instantly infatuated.'

Alewyn felt his ears burn and was glad he had left his hair down. Why he was blushing, he didn't know. Perhaps it was because Edmund had suggested he was smitten earlier. 'You offered my brother a sum of money if he promoted the match. You are from a wealthy family and so my brother agreed. Can we say you are from Northern England? I doubt Yonescu knows anyone from that part of the country. You're not the heir to your family's fortune but you're wealthy in your own right. Does that sound believable?'

Apart from the bit about him coming from the North, it was all surprisingly accurate and would not be hard for him to pretend. 'Yes. That sounds fine. Why did you agree to marry me? You seem to be a woman who enjoys being in charge. I cannot imagine you submitting to marriage because your brother thinks it is a good idea.'

He heard her inhale of surprise. 'Not many people…' she began but then she trailed off. She cleared her throat. 'I took one look at you and knew you would be a good worker. That, coupled with your wealthy family, made you an attractive proposition to me. Yonescu knows how bad things are here. He will understand my reasoning.'

Alewyn nodded, wondering what she had been going to say before she stopped herself. It would appear odd if he continued to stare at the fire and so he turned towards her. 'Why do you need more workers? This is a small stronghold and, apart from the necessary repairs, everything seems to be running smoothly.' He didn't comment on the lack of guards. As he wasn't supposed to be able to remember anything from his past life, showing knowledge of security matters was not a good idea.

She closed her ledger and rested her long fingers on top of the book. 'When my husband died, many men left to find glory elsewhere. They seemed to believe a woman would not lead them to war. I am somewhat lacking in strong men.' She glanced at his arms and he resisted the urge to flex his muscles.

'Were the men right? Are you unlikely to lead them to war?'

Lady Johanne ran her fingers along the edge of her ledger. 'War is foolish. The waste of life is senseless. If that's what the men wanted, then they were right to leave.'

His stomach tightened; she was against war.

Could this be it? And why was a heavy weight settling in his chest? If he discovered she was guilty, he could return to Windsor victorious. The knowledge should bring him joy, not dread. 'And what if King Edward goes to war with France? It is looking increasingly likely.'

She stood, moving around the desk. The sleeves of her dress brushed against his arm as she passed, sending a strange tingling sensation along his skin. He moved, allowing a gap between them.

She held out her hands towards the flames. 'Let us hope that Edward does not lead us into a pointless war. There is no need for men to die for the sake of a patch of land most of us will never see and which is of no benefit to most English people.'

Alewyn waited for her to say more. The deliberate silence was a trick he had learned from his friend Theo: leave a silence and the person you were talking to would want to fill it. He waited even longer still but Johanne said nothing more on France.

'Is there anything else you would like to know about me?' she asked when the silence became awkward.

'I...' Yes. He wanted to carry on the conversation but he didn't know how to do that without raising her suspicions. He wished he'd had more time to speak with Theo or his clever wife, before he'd left on this mission, to get some training on getting information out of people who didn't want to divulge it. He didn't know what else he could do to turn the conversation towards France and this opportunity was slipping through his fingers. 'I cannot think of anything more,' he admitted reluctantly.

She nodded. 'Then I have a few questions for you.'

He hadn't been expecting that. 'Ask away.'

'You called yourself Sir Alewyn when you introduced yourself to Morcant. Is that your real name?'

He'd forgotten he'd done that. That was a foolish mistake but he'd been unable to come up with anything else in the heat of the moment. If anyone knew of Sir Alewyn of the King's Knights, then it wouldn't be very hard to identify him. He was hardly an inconspicuous man. 'Perhaps it is my name. It sounds right. Or perhaps it is the name of someone I know.' He shrugged, aiming for a nonchalance he did not feel. 'I'm sorry, I cannot remember if it is or not.' The lie tasted bad but he was too far in to tell the truth. He hoped she believed him and didn't ask again. He couldn't take lying to her another time. She hadn't questioned him when he'd called himself Al. She was altogether too trusting and the thought made his heart ache as he gazed at the curve of her ear. He had to keep reminding himself that she might be a traitor because it was all too easy to forget that.

She twisted and turned her fingers as she held them out to the flames. He watched transfixed as she flexed them. He'd never fantasised about a woman's hands before, never really paid them much attention, but now he could picture Lady Johanne's fingers tracing slowly across his stomach, heading down…

'It's been a hard winter,' she murmured.

His brain was a fog of lust. 'Has it?'

'I'm sorry. I keep forgetting that you cannot remember anything.'

He winced, wishing she wasn't showing him so much sympathy. That kindness coupled with his out-of-control desire made him feel like a damned cur, like it wasn't her who was the potential traitor but himself. All his instincts screamed at him that she was not guilty. She was too kind, too thoughtful.

'It does not matter,' he reassured her. 'I am content here for the time being.'

'What if you already have duties? What if you could get into trouble by not being where you're supposed to be?' She glanced up at him, her blue eyes full of guilt.

'I...' He trailed off. They were so close. He could see a slight smattering of freckles across the bridge of her nose and a faint scar across the top of her eyebrow. He longed to reach out and trace the curve of her cheek. The desire that had been simmering beneath his skin for days rushed to the surface. His body tightened. She swayed towards him, her lips parting. Without thinking, his fingertips traced the back of her hand; her skin was so soft under his rough calluses. He thought she might pull away, but her thumb lightly stroked the inside of his wrist. He swallowed as sensation shot through him, far more intense than anything he had ever experienced before. Her hands turned towards his and their fingers linked. She took a step towards him. She was so tall. If he leaned closer, he could brush her forehead with his lips. He would only need to tilt his head slightly and he could claim her mouth.

Her back straightened and she stepped away from him. 'Of course. As you said, we are not going to really marry. I have no further questions for you, and if you've none for me, then we had better get back to work.'

She returned to her side of the desk and once more opened the ledger. She ran her fingers down the column she had been working on and gave every appearance of a woman deep in thought, but he could see the way her fingers trembled. She was not as unaffected by what had just passed between them as she would like him to believe.

Chapter Six

Johanne watched the flickering light playing over the candlestick at the centre of her private dining table. Her finest wares were on display. They only came out for meals with Yonescu. Johanne didn't quite know why she did it. Yonescu would be able to see from the state of the castle that Brae was not as wealthy as it once was but for some reason she tried to keep up the charade that she was as wealthy as when Badon had been alive.

Badon had had no problem taking extra tithes from the peasants who lived at Brae and farmed the lands around its walls. Only he did it, not for some essential item, only when he wanted to purchase some luxury item. Johanne didn't have it in her to do the same, even when the situation was bad. She saw how some families worked so hard and had so little and she didn't want to be part of their problem. Badon would have called her weak, but Badon was dead and she made her own decisions now.

She moved around the room, positioning a goblet to one side and then putting it back again. Behind her, Gemel shifted on his feet. 'You've been avoiding him. Do you think that's wise?'

There was no point asking about whom Gemel was talking. He'd been going on about Alewyn ever since they'd picked him up and slung him across Gemel's horse.

'I thought you wanted him gone. Now you want me to talk to him.'

'The more you talk to him, the more likely we are to find out why he is here. I find it hard to believe a man like him has just washed up on our shore.'

'We found him on the path, not the beach.'

Gemel huffed. 'You know exactly what I mean. Those clothes of his belong to a wealthy man. He is someone of importance. And that name, Sir Alewyn... I have heard it before.'

'So you've said, but you don't know where and, until you do, we have to trust that he is exactly as he seems. He is a hard worker; everyone has said so and we've both seen it. He does the work of five men.'

'Everyone believes he is about to become your husband. They are hardly likely to complain about him. Although, yes, I must concede, he does a lot of physical work without griping.'

'Mmm,' Johanne mumbled, hoping that would be the end of the conversation. She didn't want to admit how many times she had stopped to watch Alewyn at work. When he set his mind to a task, he gave himself to it with wholehearted determination. He was a brilliant worker who powered through jobs with the strength of ten men. To mention that she knew this would betray just how much interest she had in him, far more interest than she should. 'We know why he is here, Gemel. The man's lost his memory and he's staying until it comes back or someone comes to find him.'

'I don't believe it.'

Johanne's fist curled; she breathed deeply, releasing it. It was no good getting angry at Gemel; he was only fulfilling his role as advisor to her. 'You told me to trust Al.'

'I told you, you could trust him with Morcant. I don't believe Al could talk to the man the way he did and be in Morcant's employ. Morcant was shaking, although he tried to hide it.' Gemel grinned at the memory.

Johanne smiled too. 'I do wish I had seen that. Look, if he is not spying on us for Morcant, then I don't see what other reason would bring him here.'

Gemel snorted. 'Then you are not thinking clearly. There are many reasons why a man might want to hide his identity. England is on the cusp of war with France. We are on the south coast with an easy landing place for friendly and unfriendly ships to come ashore.'

'There are better places.' Although Johanne didn't know that for sure, never having gone east to Dover where it was said you could see France on a cloudless day. If France came to England, surely they would land there and not here in Brae. She was counting on it, desperate to avoid war being anywhere near her son's castle. Falling into French hands was even worse than losing the territory to Morcant. With Morcant, there was the possibility of getting it back. If the French took control, it would mean England had lost the war and nothing would ever be the same again.

'You are right,' Gemel continued. 'There

are better, nearer places to land. Dover is a prime example, and I pray every day that we can avoid war near our shores but that doesn't mean my prayers will be answered. Besides, there could be another reason for Al's appearance at Brae that doesn't involve France at all. Do you think Morcant is the only one interested in Brae's land? What's to say Al isn't from a family that's also interested? Granted, he really was unconscious when we picked him up but that doesn't mean he hasn't seen this as a golden opportunity to get close to you.'

'We've gone over this possibility. If I can hold off Morcant, then I can hold off Al. He has done nothing to suggest he is interested in making this marriage a reality.' That was not entirely true. There had been that moment when Johanne thought Al might kiss her, when his warm fingers had traced over her skin. She had leaned towards him, her body taking no heed of the warning her brain had shouted. She had wanted to feel his lips against hers. It had taken all her willpower to move away from him and return to her ledger. It had taken her the rest of the afternoon to force the memory from her mind. Now she and Gemel were talking about matters very close to it, the strange longing started up again.

'You need to be careful, Johanne,' said Gemel gently. 'I've seen the way you look at him and the way he looks at you.'

Johanne's heart leapt. She thought Al might desire her, but she hadn't realised it was obvious to other people. She fought to keep the smile off her face and then it faded altogether. The looks Gemel thought he was seeing were probably Al pretending to be her betrothed; he was a fantastic worker after all and this was part of his role. It shouldn't matter either way. 'I don't look at him any differently from how I look at any of my good workers.'

Johanne's cheeks heated as Gemel laughed. Fortunately, he didn't say anything else as the door opened and Al stepped in. Johanne's traitorous heart skipped another beat.

Gemel nodded at Al, who nodded back. The two of them rarely spoke to one another but, thus far, Gemel had been cordial towards Al.

'I will leave you to your dinner, Lady Johanne. But think on what I have said.' Gemel nodded once more in Al's direction before striding out of the room and leaving them alone.

'He does not trust me,' said Al as Gemel's footsteps faded into the distance.

'He does not.' Johanne did not see a reason to lie about it. Gemel's wariness was plain to see. Besides, it did no harm for Al to know he wasn't above suspicion.

Al nodded. He did not seem upset to have the truth confirmed. 'What does he suspect me of?'

'That you have designs on Brae.'

'I can promise you that I do not, but I would say that anyway, wouldn't I?' Al's lips turned up in a half-smile.

Johanne did not like the way her heart reacted to the sight of the lopsided grin. 'He also thinks that you could be a spy.'

Was it her imagination or did Al pale at that comment?

'Why would anyone spy on you?'

Interesting that he didn't deny it. Perhaps he was a spy, but that didn't mean he would find anything of interest at Brae. If that's why he was here, he was wasting his time. She shrugged. 'I have no idea why anyone would want to pry into my life or anyone else's at Brae. There is nothing for any self-respecting spy to find. I lead a very boring life, as does the rest of my household. Our only worry is ensuring there is enough food on the tables at the end of every day.'

'Attempts on your life are your normal everyday occurrence then?'

Johanne reached out and held on to the edge of the wooden table. 'I had forgotten I had told you about that.'

'Perhaps you could tell me about it before Yonescu arrives.'

He stepped closer towards her. Her head told her to back away but her feet refused to obey. He was wearing the clothes she'd found him in. They were far better quality than those she'd loaned him and they clung to his body like a second skin. She longed to reach out and trace her fingertips over the curves of his muscled arms but she held herself still.

'Johanne.' She startled at the sound of her name, spoken in a growl. She caught his gaze, saw her own desire reflected in his eyes. 'Johanne, when you look at me like that I… It makes me want to… I can't, even though I want…' He pushed the hair away from his forehead and paced away from her.

Johanne stood frozen in shock. She hadn't expected him to draw attention to the desire that pulsed between them, for him to bring it out into the open like that. She thought he'd be like her, that he would politely ignore it until he left Brae. It was what she was planning on doing.

'I…' She did not know what she was going to say. To apologise perhaps, or to deny it, but he waved her words away.

'I'm sorry. I shouldn't have mentioned anything.' Her heart thudded painfully. She pressed a hand to her chest. She wasn't sure whether it was from relief or disappointment. The table stood between the two of them, enough distance that she could no longer see the expression in his eyes in the candlelight. 'You were going to tell me about the attack on your life. Can you be absolutely sure it was against you personally?'

She took a deep breath, the change of conversation leaving her dizzy. 'Yes. I was riding with Gemel. We had gone to Snargate to see about a stonemason. You'll have noticed that Brae needs some repair work and none of the men here are up to the job.'

'Where is Snargate?'

'About a morning's ride away, to the north. I don't normally go so far. I don't like to leave

Cineas but the stonemason came highly rec-
ommended.'

'By whom?'

'Yonescu.'

'The man we are meeting tonight?'

'Yes.'

'And was he there, this stonemason?'

'No. We had missed him.'

'How do you know this?'

'What are you suggesting?'

Al huffed out a sigh. 'I'm not suggesting
anything. I'm trying to get the whole story. I
want to help you.'

She peered at him through the smoky haze
of the chamber. His shoulders were tense and
his line of questioning had been abrupt but she
still couldn't see how this information could be
used to his advantage. 'Very well, I'll tell you
what occurred that day, but I don't see how it
will help.' The thrum of desire was replaced
by a pulse of irritation. 'We were meant to
meet the stonemason at a tavern but when we
arrived there was no one there. Gemel and I
spoke with the tavern owner. He told us that
the stonemason had arrived a day earlier than
we'd expected. He'd waited an entire day and
then left.'

Alewyn nodded slowly. 'That is believable, I suppose.'

'You sound sceptical. I assume you think that Yonescu had something to do with it, but you don't know our background. Yonescu has been good to me ever since Badon's death; he has been nothing but supportive. There is no reason to suspect the stonemason was anything other than legitimate and that there was a confusion about the dates. Yonescu was apologetic afterwards and offered to send his own stonemason to us once he finished his latest project. And before you ask, I am expecting him to arrive in the spring.'

'I'm sorry, I did not mean to sound mistrustful. Please go on.'

She shrugged. 'There is not much more to tell you. On our way back, we were accosted by several men. Gemel may look like an old man but he was a good fighter in his day and there is still some life left in him.' Johanne inhaled deeply. She hated to think of the attack, hated to remember just how vulnerable she had felt and what she had lost. 'Gemel was able to push the men back. My...' She shook her head, frustrated as tears threatened. She was not normally given to tears. 'I lost my horse that day.

We'd been together a long time.' She brushed
a tear away. 'I don't know why I'm still upset.
Oh, there is no need…'

Al's arms came around her, pulling her
against his solid chest. The sadness she'd felt
at the memory of her beloved Bel vanished as
the stubble from his jaw brushed against her
forehead, sending waves of pleasure crashing
through her.

Even as her mind screamed at her not to, she
slipped her arms lightly around his waist, her
fingers against his back. He inhaled roughly as
her hand made contact and a thrill shot through
her. Badon had never reacted positively to her
touch, only bedding her to produce an heir.
She'd heard that the act between a man and a
woman could be pleasant, that with the right
lover she would feel things that would explain
why other people enjoyed it so much. She'd
not believed it until now. Would it really be
so wrong to go further than this, to find out
whether she could feel all those things people
talked about? If the briefest touch of his skin
against hers felt so good, how would it feel for
her whole body to be pressed against his? An
involuntary shudder rippled through her and
he tightened his grip.

'I didn't mean to upset you with my clumsy questioning. I'm sorry.' His voice rumbled in his chest beneath her ear.

She knew she should step away now. He was only holding her because he believed her still tearful but she didn't want to move from his embrace; she was fully enclosed by his arms, protected from anything outside this room.

'Can you carry on telling me what happened or would you like to stop now?'

So, he wasn't as affected by their embrace as she was. He wanted to continue talking about Morcant's attack. Later she would unpick the reason this felt strange to her but for now she would tell him what he wanted to know.

'There is not much more to tell. Gemel held the men off and I scrambled onto his horse. When there was a moment's break in the fighting, Gemel joined me and we rode away.' This simple explanation didn't convey the gut-wrenching terror of the moment, of how her arms had screamed out for her child, wanting to feel the weight of him once more before she died. She was more grateful than she could ever express for Gemel's quick thinking in that moment.

'How can you be sure Morcant was behind the attack?'

'I suppose I am not entirely sure. It's only… the men mentioned his name and…he has made no secret of his desire to get hold of Brae. An attack on me seems like a logical manoeuvre. Why? Do you think differently?'

'I think… But then… Sorry, I'm not good at this…'

'Not good at what?'

'Puzzling things out. This attack on you; it seems wrong somehow, too obvious.'

'Can you explain why?'

Beneath her ear came the steady sound of Al's heart. 'I know I've only met Morcant on that one occasion, but he came across as up-front. He wants Brae. He is not sneaky or underhand about it. He's brazen when he speaks of it. He may be trying to manipulate you by playing on your concerns about a French invasion by implying that you need a husband to protect you. But that is different from mounting a sneak attack. And the mention of his name, that seems too overt to me, as if someone said it deliberately. And…' He trailed off.

'And?'

'I'm not doubting Gemel's fighting abilities.

I'm sure he's… I mean, he looks competent, but an old man against a group of fighters.' She felt him shrug. 'If they had really wanted to kill you, I'm sure they would have done.'

They stood in silence for a while. It should have been odd, standing in one another's arms, but somehow it wasn't. 'If the point of the exercise was not to kill me, what was it?'

'I don't know,' he murmured. 'Perhaps someone is trying to scare you.' He rubbed his hand absentmindedly down her back; without thinking she arched into him. He froze. She held her breath and then gradually lifted her head until she was looking directly at him. He was gazing down at her; his eyes were almost completely black. He slowly, almost imperceptibly, lowered his head towards her. There was time for her to move away, to put a stop to this absurdity, but she didn't. Her eyes fluttered shut as his lips hovered over hers. Her heart began to beat painfully fast.

The chamber door opened with a sharp click. Al dropped his arms from around her, whirling round to face the intruder, his hand appearing to reach for a sword that wasn't there. His bulk shielded her from the newcomer but his protection wasn't necessary.

'Good eve, my friends.' Yonescu's voice sounded from in front of Al. Johanne inhaled deeply, willing her heart rate to calm down, but it was still clamouring as she stepped around Al's bulk.

'A warm welcome, Yonescu,' she said, moving towards the baron, stretching out her hands in welcome towards her neighbour.

In comparison to Al, Yonescu was a tiny man, stick-thin with very little hair; his smile, though, that was full of amusement as he looked between the two of them.

'I seem to have interrupted something; I should have knocked. Although I must say, I am pleased to see this is not a marriage of convenience.' Heat swept over Johanne's cheeks; she'd hoped Al's body had blocked his view of what Al and she were doing, but then her hands had been on his back and there was no other reason for them to be there unless... 'Ah, my dear, there is no need to blush. I am pleased to see you happy. You deserve it after so long. Let me look at your betrothed.'

Al moved forward, towering over Yonescu. To his credit, Yonescu didn't shrink at Al's approach, but then Johanne had noticed that Al never used his size to intimidate people. Oh, she had no doubt that he could—she'd witnessed it when Morcant had barged into Brae's Great Hall—but she hadn't seen him display that aggressive dominance since. He was considerate whenever he spoke to anyone smaller than himself, toning down the boom of his voice and changing his stance to appear unintimidating. He was colossal compared to most, but this wasn't a threatening situation and so his body language was that of a gentle giant.

'Sir Alewyn, allow me to introduce my closest, and by far my most supportive, neighbour, Sir Yonescu.'

The two men shook hands. 'The pleasure is all mine,' said Yonescu. 'I'm so pleased that Lady Johanne has someone to fight in her corner. Too long she has had to manage on her own.'

'I have hardly been on my own. I have Gemel…'

'An old man who is your servant is not the same as a man in his prime.' Yonescu glanced at Alewyn approvingly.

Gemel was more than capable despite his age, but Johanne did not want to get into an argument. 'Let's eat.' She gestured to the two men to take their seats at the table. 'I will let you two get to know each other while I let the kitchen know we are ready.'

Johanne stepped into the corridor and scurried away from the door. When she was sure she was far enough away she stopped and leaned against the wall, letting out a long, slow breath.

If they hadn't been interrupted, would Al have kissed her? Would she really have allowed it? She would never know. Yonescu had stopped it before it could happen, and now she was away from Al her common sense had returned. She had to have a clear head; she had to use Al to get what she wanted from him, and she had to be able to let him go when the time came for him to move on.

She pushed herself away from the wall and began to walk briskly towards the kitchen. She wanted Al and Yonescu to like each other, and nothing eased conversation better than a fine meal and some decent ale.

Days passed, or so it seemed to Alewyn, as the meal dragged on into eternity.

On the surface Yonescu was perfectly pleasant. He said everything right, repeatedly showering praise on Lady Johanne and congratulating them on their betrothal, but there was something about the man that made Alewyn's skin crawl.

Yonescu's smile, the one seemingly fixed on his face, never reached his eyes. Everything he said seemed calculated to get the best response from Lady Johanne and she lapped it up. Alewyn wasn't jealous, that wasn't the reason his stomach twisted every time Lady Johanne laughed at one of Yonescu's comments. Yonescu was an old man and not in the least attractive. There was no reason for Alewyn to feel so protective of her. The moment that had passed between him and Lady Johanne before Yonescu entered had been nothing more than a brief loss of his mind. It would not happen again. He would never take her into his arms. No, he was not jealous of the way Lady Johanne smiled at her neighbour. There was no flirtation in their interactions. Yonescu did not want Lady Johanne in his bed. That he wanted something else from her was certain. What that something was, Alewyn had no idea.

Finally, the last of the food was consumed and the table was bare. Surely, it was time for Yonescu to go but there appeared to be no sign of the evening coming to an end.

'There was another reason for me coming

here tonight,' said Yonescu as he leaned forward and rested his arms on the table.

Alewyn resisted the urge to roll his eyes. This was it, the reason behind the whole farce of the evening.

'I'm afraid I've heard some troubling news.'

Lady Johanne stilled, her fingers resting on the stem of her goblet. 'Oh?'

'Yes, I'm afraid it concerns yourself and Brae.' Yonescu seemed to be enjoying this far too much for Alewyn's taste; his eyes were glinting in the candlelight, not with amusement but with some other suppressed emotion. Alewyn wanted to reach across and shake the man. 'It's been brought to my attention that Morcant is building siege weapons.'

Lady Johanne inhaled sharply. 'Siege weapons. Are you sure?'

Yonescu gave a solemn nod that somehow didn't ring true to Alewyn. He glanced at Lady Johanne. The walls she built around her, the ones no one else other than he seemed to notice, had crumbled slightly. She was holding herself very still, but Alewyn could see the faint tremor in her jaw. Without thinking, he reached over and covered her hands with his. Her skin was icy-cold.

He wanted to rage at Yonescu, but he knew that would not be helpful. He cleared his throat. 'Siege weapons on their own do not necessarily mean anything. Every good castle should maintain their arsenal. To do otherwise, especially as England is about to go to war, would be unwise. I understand his land is not far from Dover and—'

'I hadn't finished.' The look Yonescu gave him would have frozen hell. Lady Johanne was staring at her goblet and didn't notice.

Alewyn was pleased to see the man's mask slip. Yonescu was not as pleasant as the image he was trying to present. He hoped Lady Johanne had picked up his tone but he doubted it. Her skin was pale and her fingers were rigid underneath his.

'What else is there?' Alewyn squeezed her hand tightly, trying to share his strength with her.

Yonescu glanced towards the door. 'I'm only telling you both this because we are allies, perhaps I can even hope that we are friends.' He learned forward and lowered his voice. 'I have a spy in Morcant's castle.'

Lady Johanne nodded tightly. 'It will go no further. You have our word on that.'

Yonescu glanced towards Alewyn, raising an eyebrow. 'And you?'

'Of course, you have my word on that too.' It was not a difficult promise to make. The knowledge that Yonescu had a spy in Morcant's stronghold mattered little to Alewyn. There was no need for him to share that information with anyone; besides, it would be more remarkable if Yonescu didn't have a spy in every household in the neighbouring castles. It was common practice. He glanced at Lady Johanne and his heart sank as he realised she probably didn't have a spy anywhere. She wouldn't be pale with shock if she had.

As he watched the levels of dismay play across her face, he came to a very firm conclusion. There was no way she could be the accomplished traitor Benedictus thought she was. She was too naive, too trusting. She didn't have it in her to create a plot that would bring down the King. Now, all he had to do was work out whether she knew about the plan and was involved in any way. Perhaps she was complicit because she felt she had no other option. Or perhaps she was unwittingly part of the plan; perhaps some baron was manipulating her and she was the unwitting stooge. Or maybe the traitorous plot was happening on her land and she was completely oblivious to it. She was not malicious or treacherous. Nothing like the rumours at Windsor painted her. Someone must have fabricated her reputation for their own ends.

Across the table, Yonescu was still talking. What he said next had Alewyn forgetting all about treason. 'I thank you both for your discretion. The information my spy has gathered is that Morcant is planning an attack on Brae.' Johanne's fingers twisted beneath his. He tightened his grip. To his surprise, she squeezed back; he'd thought she was barely aware of his presence. 'As you're aware,' Yonescu continued, 'Morcant has wanted Brae for some time now. We knew he thought marriage to you would be the easiest way to acquire the territory, but now that route is cut off by your recent betrothal he has decided to take much more drastic measures. He plans to lay siege to Brae soon. He believes Sir Alewyn will not have had time to create enough opposition.'

Lady Johanne sat a little taller. 'And what of my defensive plans?'

Yonescu affected a pained look which was as genuine as his fake smiles had been earlier.

'Lady Johanne, my dear, you and I have been friends for a long time. Since before your dear husband passed away. You are a kind and generous leader but you must admit that defence at Brae is woefully inadequate. You do not have the manpower necessary to shore up the level of fortification needed for you to withstand a siege.'

Lady Johanne's lips thinned and she cast her gaze downwards. Alewyn wanted to reach over the table and slam Yonescu's self-satisfied face into it, even as he agreed with Yonescu's assessment of Brae's defences. Instead, he asked, 'How long does your spy think we have?'

'Not long. Morcant is working quickly. Two weeks, maybe, definitely before spring.'

Lady Johanne groaned quietly.

Alewyn searched his mind for what Benedictus would ask at this point. His brother would have had a plan of action before Yonescu had stopped speaking but nothing was coming to mind. After a while he settled on, 'Are you sure your spy is reliable? It is odd to mount an attack during the winter.'

Yonescu glared at him once more. Alewyn supposed Yonescu was hoping Lady Johanne would respond rather than him, but words seemed beyond her now.

'Of course my man is reliable. I would not have deployed him if he were not.'

'Very well. Then on behalf of Lady Johanne and myself, I will say thank you for your kindness in letting us know about the threat to our home. I think we can both agree that Lady Johanne is not feeling well. We must give her some time to rest and think about this new development. Allow me to escort you to your horse.'

For the space of a heartbeat, Alewyn thought Yonescu would argue. He was certainly looking towards Lady Johanne as if he were waiting for her to contradict Alewyn, but she said nothing. Alewyn stood and Yonescu could do nothing but follow his lead.

Lady Johanne still hadn't said anything by the time the door closed behind them.

'I am sorry to be the bearer of bad news,' said Yonescu as they made their way through the corridors and out through the Great Hall.

Although Yonescu's words dripped with sincerity and concern, Alewyn couldn't shake off the feeling that the man wasn't being truthful. He wished he could read people as his fellow knight Theo could. Alewyn was sure Theo would know what Yonescu's motivations were just by looking at the slimy man.

'Although it doesn't seem like it, we are grateful for you coming to tell us the news. It was better we found out tonight than when Morcant is outside our walls.' Alewyn swallowed down the guilt that rose from his stomach. He would not be at Brae by the time the siege happened. If Lady Johanne proved to be guilty, then she would not be here either. And if she wasn't and he had left her alone, it would be highly unlikely Lady Johanne would last longer than a day under siege. Brae's defences were inadequate and her people were lacking in fighting capabilities.

Even in the space of a day, how many of her people would die? And what would become of young Cineas? The thought of anything hurting that small, trusting boy almost brought Alewyn to his knees. He could not think about it, could not allow himself to get any further involved in this dispute. Territory issues only came to the attention of the King's Knights if they threatened the King's interests. This tussle over land was not something that could or should concern him. France was of far greater importance.

Alewyn watched while Yonescu gathered his men together. They had been in the Great Hall, dining with Lady Johanne's people, while Gemel watched over them. Yonescu's men looked at him with respect and admiration. There were no hidden glances, no sense that Yonescu was anything other than he seemed: a decent nobleman who cared for his neighbour's safety. And yet…and yet Alewyn couldn't help but feel that there was something off about him, as if the centre of his being was somehow rotten. Was he seeing things that weren't there? Was it because he was looking for secrets when, in fact, there were none?

His head ached.

He wanted to speak with Lady Johanne, to see whether she had the same sense about Yonescu as him, but when he returned to the antechamber, she was no longer there.

Chapter Seven

It was still dark outside, not even the roosters were stirring. Johanne raised her hand, ready to knock against Al's bedchamber door. She paused before her fist connected with the wood; was she going to do this? If she did, she really was putting her trust in a man she didn't know all that well. A man she was trusting with not only her life but also all the lives of the people who called Brae their home. And yet, did she have a choice? No. She didn't.

She knocked. There was no sound from inside the chamber but that was not a surprise. Most of the castle inhabitants were sleeping. She'd have been more surprised had he answered. Normally, she too would be sleeping deeply at this hour, but she hadn't been able to relax after Yonescu had left. Every time she closed her eyes, all she could see was Morcant's soldiers outside the walls of Brae: men with swords advancing on her son's legacy. She could hear the women of the castle screaming and the sound of men dying to protect them from Morcant's assault. There was no way she could sleep, not when she should be doing something to prevent it all from happening.

Which is why she was here. Standing outside Al's chamber waiting for a response from her knock. She tried again: nothing.

She pushed open the door and stepped inside; the fire was down to its last embers, barely emitting any light, but it was enough for her to make out the shapes of the room. Deep breathing came from the mattress. She made her way over to it, where she could make out Al's bulk but not his features. One arm was thrown across his eyes. She crouched down and shook it gently.

Before she knew what was happening, strong hands gripped her. She was turned, in the air, and flipped onto her back, a heavy weight pressing her down into the mattress. All the air whooshed out of her; she couldn't breathe. Her heart raced as she struggled to get free but the hands only held her tighter; there was no way to escape.

In a moment, she was back in her marriage bed, Badon holding her down as he exerted his marriage rights. She'd never denied him, never told him no, even though she'd found the whole thing uncomfortable. It didn't matter that she had given herself willingly; he'd wanted to dominate her, even in that intimate moment when there was no one around to witness her subjugation. She blinked. Badon was dead. She was back in the chamber with Al and she had taken him by surprise.

'Let go,' she hissed, wriggling to free herself.

'Oh, it's you,' Alewyn grunted. He let go of her arms and some of the weight lifted off her. She inhaled, deeply grateful to get air into her lungs.

'You're incredibly heavy.'

'Sorry,' he muttered. He rolled off her completely and flopped backwards onto the mattress next to her.

They lay next to each other in silence. She concentrated on breathing in and out. Whenever she was reminded of Badon she needed a moment to recollect that he was no longer alive, that he could no longer control every moment of her day.

She focused on the feel of the mattress beneath her and on Al's steady presence next to her. Gradually, her heart rate returned to normal.

Almost as if he sensed she was no longer frightened, he asked, 'What can I do for you, Lady Johanne?'

She couldn't help the laugh that gurgled out of her. He was so polite, even in the strangest of situations.

The mattress shook next to her as he laughed softly with her. Her heart tightened at the sound. In the short time she'd known him, she had not seen him smile fully, only the half-smile that made her heart flutter strangely.

'I apologise for pinning you to the bed,' he said seriously when their laughter had ebbed away. 'I thought I was under attack. Why are you here?'

'I need your help with something.'

'Now?'

'Of course now.' She began to move off the mattress. She couldn't discuss her future while she could sense the weight of him next to her.

She rolled to the floor, the cold of the flag-stones shocking a gasp out of her.

'What's wrong?' His shape loomed over her.

'Nothing. It's cold. Come on. You need to get dressed.'

'Tell me what we are doing first.'

She paused. She'd spent the whole night thinking about it, she was surprised it wasn't obvious. 'We're going to Ormond.'

She heard a long exhale. 'Where exactly is Ormond?'

'It's Morcant's stronghold.'

A pause. 'You want to see the truth of Yonescu's rumours.'

'Yes.'

She heard him move from the mattress, the thud of his feet hitting the floor and the swish of cloth as he pulled on his clothes. Her heart expanded. For a moment there, she'd thought he would argue with her, but with no further questions asked he was ready and willing to help. She'd never met anyone like him.

The early-morning sky was completely clear and frost crunched underfoot as they stepped into the courtyard. It would not be an easy ride today, but she had to know if Morcant really was preparing for war. She had to know what was coming her way.

'I will fetch the stable master. He will know which of the horses will be able to carry your weight for a full day.'

Al nodded and, without comment, he made his way over to Johanne's horse and began to saddle up. She watched for a moment; his movements were precise and measured, as if he had done this many times before. She turned away from him before he could notice she was watching.

It took two attempts to wake the stable master but once he was up he helped them get ready in silence. 'Gemel's in charge today,' she told him as she vaulted into her saddle. 'I am taking Al on a tour of Brae's land.'

The man nodded sleepily before turning away from them and heading back to his bedding.

Rousing the one guard she had in place took longer than it should have done but she needed him to let them out of the castle. Al's forehead was pinched during the whole process; seeing it from his point of view she could understand why. One tired, old guard was not enough to defend Brae from a couple of angry peasants let alone a siege.

She shifted on her saddle as the portcullis rose agonisingly slowly. She didn't want to draw attention to her leaving. If questioned, she would give the same excuse she had given the stable master and her guard but she knew that not everyone would believe her. She was a terrible liar and Gemel would see through her. If the stable master reported what she was doing as fact she hoped to avoid speculation. Any rumours would be dangerous. Fear of the unknown spread quickly and was even more poisonous than reality.

'Do you think your men believe you?' murmured Al.

'I think so.'

He raised an eyebrow.

'I know, I'm a terrible liar. Gemel would have seen straight through me. I probably only got away with that because they were both half asleep.'

'Why not tell them the truth?'

'Because I want life at Brae to continue as normal for as long as possible. If the threat of a siege becomes common knowledge, then… Lots of people could leave,' she finished quietly. Brae was only existing now on a very delicate balance; anything that upset this could be catastrophic.

'I see,' was all he said in response.

Finally, the gate was raised and they were free. She kicked Heled into motion and the horse flew out of Brae's walls. Next to her, Al did the same. The ride to Ormond would take the whole morning and into the early afternoon. She wanted to reach there while it was light enough to see what was going on within the grounds of Morcant's castle.

For a while they rode in silence. Now that she was doing something, calm was settling in and the fear she'd felt while lying alone was beginning to dissipate. If Morcant was planning a siege against her, knowing about it would give her time to plan. She would not go down without a fight.

It was still dark when Alewyn broke the silence. 'Why are you not taking Gemel with you today instead of me?'

'Gemel is old. He would not be able to manage the trip in a day.'

There was silence. 'What are the other reasons?'

She paused for a moment and then shrugged.

What did it matter if Al knew the whole truth? 'If anything happens to me, I trust that Gemel will keep Brae safe for Cineas.'

'And…'

'I trust that you will be better at protecting my body than an old man.'

'Is that all?'

Not quite. She'd wanted to spend the day with him without the distraction of everyday life getting in the way. That she could only just about confess it to herself; no one else would ever know. 'That is all.'

Thankfully he did not push her any further.

Their horses ate up the distance. The sun began its slow climb over the horizon as their horses' hooves pounded along the track.

'Why do you trust me? I could be in league with Morcant for all you know.'

She glanced across at him. 'Are you?'

'If I were, I would hardly confess it to you, would I?'

There was the half-smile on his lips, the one that made her heart tighten, the one that she wanted to touch. She looked away from him towards the horizon. 'I don't see why you would be working for Morcant. Gemel told me that although he tried to hide it, Morcant was terrified of you. He would not want someone working for him who was more physically dominant than he is. Also, I don't think he would be subtle enough to employ a man to infiltrate my castle to gain my trust. I don't see what he would gain from your presence at Brae.'

He appeared to ponder this for a moment. 'I agree. If the rumour of the siege is true, then he is a man with a far blunter method for subduing his enemies than simple spying.'

'True.' She almost laughed before she remembered why they were on this journey. 'Do you think there is any possibility the siege is a tall story?' She hated the desperate hope she could hear in her own voice, hated that she didn't have the confidence she needed to show at this moment.

'I hope it is a rumour.' He pushed his hair from his forehead. 'Brae is not strong enough to withstand an attack, even if we work all day and night for the next month repairing the walls and creating our own weapons.'

Al's words hit her like a blow to the stomach. It was nothing she had not thought of herself but to hear someone else voice her concerns…that was bone-weakeningly awful. 'Do you really think there is nothing we can do, nothing that can prevent the worst from happening?'

'I... I... Let us hope Yonescu's report is wrong. It is always possible for news to become twisted in the telling but... I think we... I mean, you must prepare for the worst.'

Johanne tried to swallow past the lump in her throat.

'I have been dreading this for years.'

'You thought Morcant might attack before now?'

'Not Morcant specifically.' The thought that someone might try and take Brae from her by force had been a constant worry ever since her husband had died.

'Why do you think no one has before now?'

'Probably because they were still too in awe of Badon's dominant personality. When he was alive, no one dared cross him, not even on the smallest matter.'

'Has anyone threatened you before?'

'Threatened, no. But there have been other things...' As the years passed, Badon's legacy had faded. Gradually, neighbouring barons had got in touch with her, offering their support in one way or another. She'd been very naive before that, thinking that married men would uphold the oaths they had made before God. Now she knew that most men were not kind. They would offer her support in exchange for the use of her body. She would not subjugate herself like that again.

'I see.' Al's voice was grim. She glanced across at him. His lips were thin, his frown deep. He very clearly disapproved. She didn't need his approval but for some reason she wanted it.

'I didn't take anyone up on their offer.'

His jaw dropped. 'I never imagined that you did.'

'Oh. You looked very fierce. I thought—'

'Not at you. At the men who... No man should offer support in exchange for...' He waved his arms around.

She smiled. 'No. I agree.'

A light dusting of pink covered his cheeks and she bit the inside of her mouth to stop herself from laughing out loud. She would never have imagined that the large man would get embarrassed talking about sexual relations.

'Yonescu was different. He was the only baron who offered me friendship without any attachment.' Although last night had been different. She had sensed an undertone to him that had never been present before. The only difference in their circumstances had been Al's brooding presence at the table. She turned to him. 'What do you think of Yonescu?'

'I think he is a self-interested, insincere, conceited bore.'

That startled a laugh out of her. 'Really?'

'Yes.'

She pondered that for a moment. 'He was different last night. Not himself. Perhaps it was the weight of the news hanging over him.'

'I don't think that was it. He struck me as insincere the moment he started congratulating us on our betrothal. Yes, he was smiling and saying all the right things, but I don't think he's pleased about the development.'

She'd had that sense too but why, she didn't know. Yonescu had been married for many years and had shown no indication that he was unhappy with the arrangement. He did not want Johanne for himself. 'What made you think he is unhappy about our betrothal? Our pretend betrothal,' she corrected.

'I…' He shrugged. 'I… I don't know, it was just a feeling I had, but I wouldn't rely on that. I don't know the man. If you think he is genuine, then…'

Johanne waited but he didn't seem to have anything more to say.

They rode in silence as the morning crept on, a tight ball of dread curling in her stomach. Was Al right? Could Yonescu have been insincere all this time? But to what end? He had never offered to warm her bed in exchange for protection or suggested that he wanted anything from her that she wasn't willing to give. She'd thought that meant she could trust him because what else could he want from her, if not her alliance?

All this time, she had believed Yonescu to be her ally. If he was as insincere as Al thought, then she truly had no one on her side. She was completely alone in the world because her brother wouldn't lift a finger to help her unless he thought he would be rewarded financially. Her finances were so meagre that she could not pay him for help. Al was here now but he would not be with her for ever.

If, by some miracle, she and Brae survived the siege she would still have to continue to live in a world where there was no one around to protect her, no one to stop any other baron from seeing what Brae had and trying to take it.

'I'd like to stop.' She brought Heled to an

abrupt halt. Not waiting to see whether Al had followed her lead, she jumped down and moved towards the edge of the path. Panic was clawing at her now, threatening to burst out of her skin and consume her. The breathing exercises that normally calmed her would not come.

She wanted to scream at the sky, to tear down the world and watch it burn. At least then it would match the feelings burning within her.

'Johanne.' Al's voice sounded behind her.

She didn't turn to him. Getting air into her body was all she could manage right at this moment.

'Johanne.'

'I don't know...' She couldn't finish the sentence. Strong arms came from behind her and wrapped her in a full body hug. She twisted and leaned into Al's firm body as his hands stroked circles around her back, the gesture reassuringly warm. He didn't say anything, didn't try to tell her that everything would be fine. She was oddly grateful.

Before Al's arrival, no one had ever held her like this, not her parents and certainly not Badon. It was always she who gave support, she never received it. She was becoming used to being comforted by him and that was not good and yet she couldn't bring herself to pull away. Right at this moment she felt safe and secure, protected from whatever evils the world threw at her.

Her heart rate began to slow, the trembling running through her subsiding as she managed to get her body under control. To stand in his embrace any longer was wrong, especially after she'd promised herself last night nothing would happen between them. She pushed at his chest and he dropped his arms. She immediately missed his warmth but to step back into his embrace would be strange, so she moved further away, putting distance between them.

'I'm sorry, I have not felt that overwhelming sense of panic in a long time.' She moved past him towards Heled but he reached out and grabbed her arm, lightly so it didn't hurt but enough that she came to a stop.

'It is understandable to feel worried at this time. You do not have to hide your emotions from me.'

She turned her back to him, shaking her head. She'd been hiding her emotions for so long now years and years had gone by of her trying to keep everything she was thinking, everything she was feeling, hidden from those around her. She was not used to sharing anything. But…what did it matter if she told Al? He was only in her life for a brief time; when he got his memory back or someone came to claim him, he would be gone from her life for ever. There was something liberating in the knowledge that she could tell him things she had told no one before and that he wouldn't hold them against her.

She rested her hand against Heled's flank. 'I don't want to let Cineas down. He's so innocent and he trusts me completely. He doesn't know it but he is relying on me to protect his heritage and I… I feel as if every day I could lose it. If I make the wrong decision and it's gone, and that feels…feels…' She touched her chest. There was a pain there, which never completely disappeared, not even when everything was going well.

Al stepped towards her. 'The only way you could let your son down is if you stop loving him. He is young. At this moment, the only thing he wants is your attention.'

'Yes, but when he is older…if he is not Baron of Brae, he will know, know that I have failed him. His father was right, I am not worthy.'

She felt, rather than saw, Al still.

'What do you mean by that?'

'Badon, Cineas's father, he…'

'He what?'

'He thought that I wasn't strong enough to be a mother of a fierce warrior. He told me that I would let Cineas down. He was very… His word was law, not just as the lord and master of Brae but of everything. Most of the time, I found him ridiculous. He was so overblown in his belief of his own self-worth. He thought everyone was weaker than him and, quite often, he was right.

'He was a big man?'

'Not particularly, at least not in comparison with you. No, it was not a physical strength he was talking about. His personality was very dominant. If he was in the Great Hall, no matter how crowded it got, you would know he was there by the sheer force of his presence. Men flocked to him and women adored him. He had to choose a wife and he wanted a treaty with my brother, whose land is in a strong position for trade. I was of a decent age and so he married me. I don't think he would have looked twice at me if it hadn't been for the agreement.

There were other women who were far more suitable to his tastes.

'When I first met him, I was so scared. I think that was what repelled him the most. He never really got over that antipathy. No matter how hard I tried to hide my nervousness from him. By the end of his life, I'd pretty much succeeded in appearing indifferent but by then it was too late. He despised me and went out of his way to make my life difficult. For the first year of my son's life, he hardly let me see him.' Pain rippled through her at the memory of those awful twelve months when it had felt like her soul was dying. She swallowed. 'Badon was worried, you see, that my weakness would rub off on Cineas, that just by being in my presence he would become scared. It took me a while but that was when I learned to toughen up, at least on the outside. I had to show Badon that I was good enough for our son. And yet, after all that, it would seem that Badon was right. I am not strong enough.'

'The late Baron of Brae sounds like a dullard.'

She surprised herself by laughing. 'Well, yes, underneath all that bluster, he was a rather dull man. He was only ever interested in being the best at everything. And if he couldn't…'

'I don't mean that he was a bore, although I am sure that he was. I mean that he was clearly lacking in intelligence. How long has he been dead?'

'Nearly three years.'

'And in all that time, you have kept Brae going. Kept the inhabitants fed and a roof over their heads.'

'Yes, but—'

'You have raised your son to be courteous and polite and yet you have also maintained his curious nature. He is well-liked among the folk who live at Brae.'

'Yes, but that is all because of his personality.'

'You cannot have it both ways, Johanne. You cannot simultaneously ruin him and claim all that is good about him is because of his natural personality. He is a good person because you have raised him to be. If you lose Brae, it will not be because you have not tried to keep it. He will be raised to be proud of his mother, a woman who faced her challenges head-on and who did not cower behind anyone. You are far stronger than you give yourself credit for and

Badon was a simpleton for not realising what an asset his wife was. Now, have you finished wallowing in self-pity? Because if you have, I understand we still have a lot of ground to cover today and we had better get moving.'

Johanne nodded, slightly stunned at what had just passed between them. Al had not spoken to her like that before, so in control and forthright. She knew what he had said was important but there was no time to think about it in detail. Later, she would turn everything over in her mind and decide whether what he said was true.

They said nothing more as they clambered back onto their horses. As the morning passed in a blur of bare trees and endless muddy paths, they spoke of little but the journey. Johanne was relieved he didn't press her for more. The words he'd spoken had shaken her. He'd been so passionately supportive of her, slightly rude, yes, but he'd said more positive things about her in that one speech than anyone had ever said about her.

The weak winter sun had just passed overhead when she pulled her horse to a stop. 'We are nearly there.'

'What is your plan?'

'Wait until dusk and then approach the castle. The gates should still be open but hopefully it will be dark enough for us to slip in unnoticed.'

She nudged Heled in amongst the trees. It was darker under their long-fingered branches and she tugged her cloak tighter around her as coldness seeped into her bones.

'I don't think that's a good idea.'

'We can't take the horses with us. We might as well storm into Morcant's Great Hall and announce our presence.'

'No. I don't think it's a good idea to try and slip into the castle grounds after dusk. If we don't find what we are looking for in a very short space of time, we are liable to be locked into the grounds for the night and run the risk of being caught.'

This was true. 'What do you suggest?'

'Ideally, I would go alone. No one other than Morcant has seen me but…' He held up a hand before she could speak. 'I know you will not be keen on that idea. I understand that you need to see the weapons for yourself in order to believe in them. Is there a settlement at Ormond?'

'Yes. The whole place is bigger than Brae,

which is why I cannot understand his desire to add Brae to his lands, as he has enough.'

'Have you visited much?'

'Once, when I was first married to Badon.'

'You are unlikely to be recognised then, unless we attract the attention of Morcant or one of his personal guards. We'll head to the tavern, there's bound to be one. We're unlikely to be asked who we are, but we can pose as husband and wife if needs be. There is no need for us to stay the night but at least the horses will get a decent rest and we can get some food.'

'What good will that do us? We need to get into the grounds. I need to see if there are weapons being assembled.'

'If weapons are being assembled, there will not be a single soul who is not talking about it, in some way or another. You would be amazed at how much it is possible to learn from idle gossip.'

'Gossip does not make it truth.'

'No. But it is a good place to start.'

She pondered his words for a moment. Her stomach growled, deciding the matter for her. She could not make that return journey without eating something.

'Very well. I agree to your plan.' She turned

Heled and followed Al back out of the forest. As they rode the rest of the way to Ormond, her thoughts turned to what had just passed between them. The way he had spoken about getting information hinted at a past where gaining hidden knowledge was important. The question was, had that come from a memory or was it instinct? If it was from memory, what else from his past did he remember? What was he not telling her?

The sweet smell of logs burning reached them as they drew nearer to the settlement. 'There's nothing so welcoming as a good fire on a winter's evening,' Al commented as they rode on. It was a throwaway comment but again it was a revelation. Was it another indication of a memory or a simple observation? She would hold off questioning him for now—discovering what was going on at Morcant's stronghold was more important—but when they returned to Brae, they were going to need a serious conversation about his memory.

'I agree. I will be grateful to get off Heled for a while.'

Al grunted in agreement and pushed on towards the settlement and the tavern they both hoped was there.

* * *

Johanne entered the inn while Al dealt with the horses in the inn's small stables. She was grateful for a moment to herself. She took a seat at the back of the room, the wood scraping against the floor as she pulled the chair away from the table. A few patrons lifted their heads at the noise but none of them seemed worried by a stranger in their midst.

'What can I do for you?'

She looked up to see an elderly innkeeper smiling down at her.

'Do you have any food?'

'Aye, I can do you some stew. And some for your strapping husband?'

So, nothing went unnoticed in this settlement. She hadn't noticed the innkeeper watching them while she was outside. 'Um, yes... yes, thank you.' She smiled, hoping she looked natural.

'Will you be needing a room for the night?'

A night spent in a room with Al was not a good idea, not when desire for his body rippled beneath her skin. Not when he had treated her with such respect and made her feel as if she were worthwhile. She was in danger here and not just from Morcant. 'No. I think we will press on with our journey after we have rested for a while.'

'Where are you heading?'

'We are on our way to Brae. My husband has family there.'

Was it her imagination or did the landlord pause? 'Right you are. Two stews are on their way.'

Johanne could tell the moment Al stepped into the taproom. Where hardly anyone had paid attention when she'd entered, the hum of voices all but stopped as heads turned towards the front of the room. More than one man reached to his side; Johanne saw the glint of metal as one went so far as to pull a dagger out and lay it on his lap.

She stood. 'There you are.' She made her way towards him and slipped her hand into his; his warm hand dwarfed hers and she ignored the tingling sensation where their skin touched. 'I was about to eat two bowls of stew myself.'

He laughed and it amazed her that she could tell the sound was false. How well she already knew him when they had not long been acquainted. 'It is a good job I came when I did. I am famished after that long ride.'

She tugged him towards the table. 'I have

already told the innkeeper that we are going to try and finish our journey to Brae today and turned down a bed for the night. You should rest now, while you can.' There, that sounded wifely and unthreatening enough.

They sat at the table. Al faced the room and she moved her chair close to his, giving every impression of a loving couple but affording her a good view of the room too. She kept her hand in his, not yet ready to relinquish the strength his touch gave her. He didn't let go either, so perhaps there was something about her touch he enjoyed or perhaps he was putting on a show for the patrons. Whatever was happening, it worked. Most hands moved away from blades, all but the dagger on one man's lap. She didn't have long to think about it before two steaming bowls of stew were placed in front of them and they dropped their contact to eat.

'Did you see the blades?' she murmured as the landlord retreated.

'Mmm,' he responded around a mouthful of food. He swallowed. 'You reacted well. I'd like to think they would have waited to see if I was threatening before stabbing me, but hopefully your timely intervention prevented the worst from happening. I would hate to fight anyone on an empty stomach.' He winked at her and she smiled at his attempt to lighten the mood. 'Is it too much to hope that the landlord told you anything about Brae when you mentioned that was where we were headed?'

'I thought he hesitated but he didn't say anything so perhaps I imagined it.'

Al shook his head. 'You have good instincts. If you thought he paused, then he did. I presume you have coins on you.'

'Of course.'

'Can you afford to be generous?'

Heat coursed across her skin. 'Not outstandingly so.'

Al took no notice of her blush. 'It does not have to be monumental. No one knows you are the Baroness of Brae here. But if we pay more than we owe and are generally well-mannered, then we might warrant a warning. You would not let someone you like head towards a siege if you could help it.'

She nodded. 'Parting with the money will be worth it if we find something out.'

The landlord returned as they finished their meal. 'How was it?' he asked as he collected their bowls.

'Delicious.' Al smiled openly at the man.

'Just what we needed after travelling all day, wasn't it, my dear.' Johanne nodded enthusiastically. 'How much do we owe?'

The landlord named a price. 'My dear, could you pay the man, please.' Al smiled at her, giving every appearance of being completely relaxed.

Johanne rummaged around in the purse strapped to her belt. Al said to offer more than the cost but she didn't want to give more than she could afford. She had very few coins on her and even those she would prefer not to part with. Almost everything she had was to be spent on repairs to Brae. Sweat broke out across her skin as the coins seemed to slip away from her. She finally settled on an amount and handed it over.

She wiped her palms on her cloak as her stomach roiled. She was not cut out for this.

The landlord flicked his gaze over the money, merely thanking her politely before moving away to speak to another customer.

'What good has that done me, other than lighten my load for the journey home?' she hissed, furious with Al. She could ill afford to lose that amount.

'Not all moves pay off straight away.' Al

took a sip of ale and looked so calm Johanne
wanted to shove him off his seat.

'It had better pay off soon because otherwise you are going to have to steal it back.'

He spluttered on his mouthful. 'I'm not sure
I'm built for stealth.'

'Hmm, we'll see. Alternatively, we could
sell that buckle.' She nodded to the clasp at
his throat. 'I'm sure that will keep us in bribes
for a while.'

He touched the silver, running his fingers
over it. He opened his mouth as if to speak but
no words came out. He dropped his hand and
picked up his tankard again.

Johanne's heart clenched. 'I'm sorry, that
was insensitive. It's probably the only connection you have with your past.' When he
still didn't say anything but continued to sip
his drink, she added, 'I really didn't mean it.
I don't expect you to sell your belongings to
help me.'

'If it helps, I will sell it,' he said gruffly, not
meeting her gaze. 'It is meaningless to me.'

'It won't come to that.' She said it brightly,
but the atmosphere between them had changed.
His mood had darkened. He continued to drink
his ale, but he was staring into the middle

distance as if his mind were elsewhere. She shifted in her seat, itching to leave the tavern, to get going and put this awkward moment behind her.

There was no way on God's earth the woman sitting next to him was a traitor to the Crown. Alewyn had thought it before but now he was sure. It just wasn't possible that someone so sweet and kind was capable of such treachery. The way she had paled when she thought he'd taken offence to her suggestion of selling the silver clasp had his stomach twisting with disgust at himself. She trusted that he was telling the truth. She had taken him in, probably saving his life in the process, and he was spying on her.

The way her fingers had trembled as she'd searched through her paltry collection of coins had hurt his heart. Despite being the caretaker of her son's castle, she had almost nothing and yet she was feeding and clothing him and giving him shelter, expecting only his support in return.

This woman lived and breathed Brae's safety; she would not risk it by smuggling Frenchmen into the country. She would not risk leaving

Cineas without her protection. She was devoted to that boy in a way that Alewyn had never experienced for himself. His parents had only ever seen him as an asset. Their validation and attention only given when he did something they approved of but readily taken away when he didn't.

They would not approve of his actions right now. They would have had him arrest Johanne on the day they met and ask her questions later. They would tell him he was not being logical, that he was not relying on evidence and that he was not a true Monceaux, who used their power to get results. And yet, all his instincts screamed at him that she was innocent.

If there were men coming into the country via the coast at Brae, then someone other than Lady Johanne was responsible. Now, all he had to do was prove it before Benedictus came swooping down from Windsor to arrest her. He swallowed as images of Lady Johanne being clamped in irons assailed him. He could not let that happen.

He glanced at the landlord. It seemed his hunch wasn't paying off. The man was deep in conversation with another patron and hadn't spared them a glance. Lady Johanne had wasted her coins for nothing and it was all his fault. 'Are you finished?'

She jumped at the sound of his voice and he cursed himself. He'd spoken harshly, acting as if she were to blame for something when the whole problem was caused by him. 'I'm ready.'

Alewyn made a show of getting to his feet, stretching and groaning as he moved, hoping to draw the landlord's attention to them. Lady Johanne sent him a look of alarm but made no comment. He was rewarded for his theatrical display by the appearance of the landlord at his side. 'Are you leaving so soon?'

Alewyn rubbed the small of his back. 'We'll stay awhile. I cannot get back on the horse until I have stretched my legs. We do not wish to trouble anyone—where do you suggest we walk so as not to alarm the townsfolk?' He smiled, hoping he looked rueful. 'I am afraid, with my size, I tend to do that without trying.' He must have pulled off the bashful look because a few of the nearby patrons chuckled and the landlord grinned.

'You could take the path to the stream,' the landlord said. 'It would give you a chance to fill up your water skins. I'll come outside with you now and show you the way.'

No one seemed to question the landlord leading them outside; most people had already returned to their conversations and didn't watch the strangers leaving the taproom. There was no hostility from the ones that watched but still Alewyn's muscles tensed. He doubted he would be able to relax, even for a moment, until they were far away from Morcant's lands.

'It is a shame it is winter; the walk is pleasant in the summer. It's a favourite with courting couples.' The landlord grinned at them and Alewyn felt heat cross his face. He was trying very hard not to think of courting and Johanne in the same sentence. 'If you step away from the inn, I'll be able to show...' The man stopped a little way from his inn and turned to face them. His genial smile had gone, replaced with a small frown. 'You seem like a decent couple and so I wanted to warn you, although many would say it is not for me to do. Still, I am a God-fearing man and I do not want it on my conscience.' Having said his piece, the landlord looked around. Lady Johanne shot Alewyn a quick glance and he tried not to preen. He had been right about the coins after all. Once the landlord was satisfied no one was around, he leaned forward towards them both. 'It is not safe to travel to Brae.' He straightened, his eyes once more darting down the empty street.

The small hairs on the back of Alewyn's neck stood on end as he forgot all about being right. 'Why is that?' he asked softly.

The landlord stepped closer still. 'Lord Morcant, the baron here at Ormond, is planning a siege on the settlement.' Next to him, Alewyn heard Johanne's soft gasp. 'He—' the landlord rolled his eyes '—the baron, that is, has plans to increase his power over the South and currently Brae only has a woman leader, so he believes he will easily be victorious. Whether he will succeed is another matter but I would hate to see you walking into a battle you could avoid. Perhaps you could visit your family another time.'

Alewyn froze. Why had he not asked what story Johanne had given to the landlord before he had joined her? He did not want to say anything that contradicted what she'd said in the inn. Sweat beaded across his brow, which he hoped the landlord would put down to fear of the siege and not because he was a thoughtless oaf.

When he said nothing, Johanne spoke, her

voice flat and lifeless. 'Thank you for your kind warning. We will be grateful for ever.'

'Yes,' Alewyn agreed. 'Thank you.'

The landlord nodded, apparently satisfied that he had done all he could. 'If you still wish to visit the stream, then follow this street until you come to the end. Once there, you will see a dense woodland; skirt around the edge of that and you will be able to hear the stream. Follow the noise. Be quick or you will lose the light altogether and will find yourselves washed away. If that is all, my friends, then I must return to my duties.'

They both thanked him again and he nodded before heading back towards the warmth of his inn. They stood motionless until the door had closed behind him.

Johanne turned to him, her face deathly pale in the fading light. 'It's true. I can't...'

Her legs buckled. Alewyn caught her before she fell to the ground. For all her long limbs, she weighed virtually nothing. Glancing around the near empty street, he spotted a narrow alleyway slightly further ahead. He carried her there, gently setting her on the ground when he was sure there was no one else around.

'My people…my son… They will all…'

'It will be all right, Johanne.' How, he didn't know. But he would do everything in his power to make sure Brae did not fall to Morcant.

'How can you say that? It cannot be all right. You have seen the people of Brae. We cannot survive an attack. The only men I have are old or not built for fighting. We will be slaughtered. We cannot win.'

'We can and we will,' said Alewyn firmly. 'I will help rebuild your defences and create the weapons you need. You are not alone in this.'

'Oh, Al, you are wrong. I am always alone.'

He shouldn't promise to help her, not when his duties could call him away at any moment, but his heart would not listen to his practical side. 'You are not alone this time.'

Chapter Eight

Despite his solemn statement, Johanne was still trembling. They were so close he could feel the vibrations against his body. He wished there was something he could do to make her feel better.

'I need to see what Morcant is planning for Brae,' she whispered.

'Yes. We should find out what we are up against.' He was aware of what he was promising. He was committing to help her, committing to support her against Morcant before he had proof that she was innocent of treason. If Benedictus were here to see him, then he would be disapproving. His displeasure would be worse than anything Alewyn had experienced before from him or their parents, and yet, saying that he would help her felt right. It *was* right. Whatever happened, he would be protecting the people he had come to know and whose company he enjoyed. But he must be honest with himself, even if he never admitted it out loud: it was Johanne herself whom he wanted to keep safe. Johanne whom he couldn't bear to let down.

'It's dark enough, let's approach the castle and see if the light is passable enough for us to make out some details.'

'Yes, yes.' She moved away from him and he immediately missed the feel of her body so close to his. But it wasn't just her physical presence she withdrew from him. He saw the effort it took to drag herself back together, saw the shields she pulled around her, the ones she wore every day and which most people saw as the real her. But it wasn't. That was what Alewyn was learning as he spent more time with her. She may present a confident front to everyone but it was a performance worthy of the most talented court jester. She was far more vulnerable on the inside than anyone other than himself suspected. That was the person he wanted to see, to spend more time getting to know.

'Let's go.' She turned towards the castle. He

knew she would expect him to follow. That she was putting on this show of confidence for him. It hurt that she felt she needed to portray that side of herself to him, that she didn't trust him enough to admit that she was vulnerable. But then, he was hiding his real self from her so he couldn't really complain. He let out a long breath; when had life become so complicated? Since he'd met Johanne, that's when.

He followed her. The feeble sun was disappearing over the horizon and soon the day would fade into darkness. The moon was already out, edged by wisps of cloud. It would give them just enough light to see but hopefully not too much for them to be seen.

He caught up with her. 'We don't want to approach by the path.'

'Oh. Of course. I don't know what I was thinking.' She veered off the well-worn track and almost walked straight into a stable. He caught her arm and pulled her out of the way before she could hurt herself.

'Calm down, Johanne. People make mistakes when they are upset and panicking. We don't want to do anything to draw attention to ourselves.'

'I'm not panicking.' The rapid rise and fall of her chest suggested otherwise.

'Let's move behind the stables here and come up with a plan.'

'We have a plan. We are going to the castle to see what is going on up there.'

He almost laughed but managed to stop himself. 'We cannot barge through the castle gate. Morcant's guards will spot us immediately and everything will be lost before we've properly begun.'

She was silent for a moment. Now the light was gone, he could not see the fine details of her face, but her tilted head suggested she was pondering his words. He did not rush her; she needed this time to regain her composure.

In the end, he had no verbal confirmation that she was happy to follow his suggestion, just a nod of the head and a quick turnaround as she headed into the darkness behind the building.

'What's your plan?' she whispered when they were safely off the path and hidden in the darker shadows.

'We approach the castle from the side and make our way around slowly and carefully. We must be wary of any footsteps heading our way. If we hear anything, and I mean anything at all, then we melt into the darkness without a word. Is that clear?'

'Yes.'

Alewyn paused for a moment. He'd had many recruits who said they understood how to be stealthy but had failed when put to the test. Should he stress it again? No, he could sense that her patience was wearing thin. If Johanne made a noise, he could always throw her over his shoulder and make away with her.

'Why are we walking around the outside of the castle and not approaching the gate?'

'We are looking for any concealed entrance or any disrepair we can exploit to get in that way.'

'All right. Let's go.'

He reached out and grabbed her arm again. 'I'm going first.'

'No. It should be me who leads the way. You are here because I forced you to come with me. Brae is my responsibility and so I should be the one risking myself.'

'That's very honourable, but not true. You didn't force me to come. You asked. You couldn't force me to do anything I didn't want to. The reason I will go first is that I am more likely to be able to overpower a guard should we stumble on one. It would be difficult for me to attack someone if your body is in my way.'

She let out a huff of impatience. 'Very well. You can lead but let's start now. The longer I wait, the sicker I'm feeling.'

'Come.' He didn't return to the path. Even in the deepening darkness it was impossible to miss the imposing walls of Morcant's stronghold, and away from the main thoroughfare was safer.

They approached the stronghold in silence, the steep incline quickening Johanne's breath as she struggled to keep pace with him. At the castle walls, he pointed towards the left and she nodded. They carried on walking; in fairness to Johanne, she was quieter than the recruits Alewyn had dealt with in the past. He could barely hear her as they moved along. High above them they heard the occasional rumble of conversation or the clink of chain mail scraping along stone. Castle Ormond was better defended than Brae, which meant more manpower for Morcant's intended siege.

They'd skirted half the castle when Alewyn came to a stop. Johanne gently bumped into him, but he caught her before she stumbled to the ground.

'Ormond is in better shape than Brae,' she whispered into his chest. 'We are not going to find a way in, are we?'

'It's not looking likely, but I've had another idea.' She muttered something so low he couldn't hear it. He decided not to follow it up. 'Can you hear that?'

She stepped a little away from him. 'Do you mean the running water?'

'Yes. The river the innkeeper was telling us about must be nearby. During a siege the castle inhabitants would want access to that fresh water. There may be a disguised entrance near the stream. I think we should at least investigate the possibility. It means moving down, away from the castle wall and into that woodland.' He nodded towards the dark outline of the trees below them.

'If it exists, how will we find it in the darkness?'

'I'll be honest, I don't know if we will but it is our best option. We cannot stroll through the front gates and we cannot climb this wall or break through it. Even if a hidden entrance exists and even if we find it, the chances of getting through it are not great. It is most likely to be barricaded in some way; there could even be a guard. You need to accept that we might not get a look at the weapons Morcant is assembling.' He paused but she didn't respond. 'I really think this idea has the best odds at being successful. Even if those odds are vanishingly small.'

He felt, rather than saw, her laugh. 'What's so funny?'

'Nothing. I don't know why I am laughing. It's better than crying, I suppose. It's all awful but at least you have not tried to placate me with false assurances. Lead me to the water.'

He held out a hand and she slipped her hand into his grip. His heart squeezed at the contact; he liked holding her hand far more than he wanted to admit.

The sound of the stream kept changing; sometimes it sounded as if it were coming from the left, other times from the right. Johanne kept her hand in his as they slipped and slid along the muddy ground. Behind him, she was starting to shiver. They would have to give up soon, but for some reason he couldn't find it in himself to voice the words; he couldn't bear the thought of disappointing her.

'I think we are getting nearer the water.' Her voice came out as a whisper, even though they were quite far from the castle and no one could hear them.

'I think you are right.' They rounded a bend and stopped just in time to prevent either of them falling headfirst into the river, which was suddenly gushing in front of them. In the light of the moon, he could make out the white of the foam as it rushed over rocks.

'What are we looking for?' Johanne twisted around, staring along the riverbed and back.

'Anything that looks vaguely like it shouldn't be here, a mound of earth or something similar. There's nothing around here…'

She nodded and together they walked on.

Johanne could barely remember a time when she wasn't sliding about in mud. Her boots were thick with it, and the hand which wasn't clutching Al's was wet with it. She wanted this relentless slog through the mire to be over, but she knew she couldn't leave until she'd seen the weapons being constructed to destroy her home. Although it might not help to see them, it couldn't be worse than her imagination.

Beside her, Al was a steadying presence.

For a woman who had sworn never to depend on anyone at all, she was relying heavily on him. It should frighten her but it didn't. Maybe because there were so many other things to worry about. Her mind could only be anxious about one thing. And yet, she didn't think that was it. Deep down, she trusted Al. She knew she would have to think about this later, to ask herself why him when she knew nothing about his background. Why him when his size should intimidate her? Why him when she barely trusted anyone else? Right now, she didn't have the energy in her to question her reasoning. Now she needed to concentrate on getting through the rest of tonight.

Her foot caught on a tree root and she stumbled. Al stopped her from falling to the ground, but a sharp pain shot up her arm. She gasped.

'Are you all right?' His other arm came around her waist, holding her tightly.

'Yes.' It was only a pain in her arm; it was nothing in comparison to the ache in her heart.

'I'm sorry, I didn't mean to tug you so quickly but I was hurrying. I think I might have found something.'

Her heart quickened. 'You have?'

'Mmm. Over there.'

He pointed to a dark shape a little further on, before slipping his arm around her waist again. It was as if he wanted to hold her as much as she valued his touch.

'It looks like a black blob.'

Laughter rumbled through him. Her heart lifted at the sound. He sounded a lot more positive than he had before they had started this absurd journey. 'Let's investigate.'

The dark shape proved to be a cave. 'Do you think this is it?'

'I think this is the best chance we've had. If it's not this, then I think we will have to head back to the tavern and rethink our strategy.'

'But I—'

'I understand how you feel, Johanne. But blundering around in the darkness is not going to help Brae. Brae will need you rested and thinking clearly if you are to plan your counter-attack.'

She hated to admit that he was right and so she kept silent.

Without saying another word, they stepped inside the shallow cave. The darkness was absolute.

'Wait here. I'll see if this leads anywhere.'

For the first time since they'd started their

exploration, he dropped her hand. She missed the contact instantly and then chastised herself. Relying on him to help her discover the extent of Morcant's arsenal was one thing, depending on the strength of his body was quite another. Before today, she would have said that Cineas's touch was the only one she truly enjoyed. The way his little arms clung to her whenever they were in private brought her a joy she had never expected in her life. To find that she welcomed the touch of another person, one who wasn't even related to her, was not something she wanted.

Her husband had used his body to dominate her. From the first day of their marriage, he had never missed an opportunity to demonstrate his superior strength over her. He rarely hit her. He hadn't had to. She'd been in such awe of him that she had obeyed him without question. She had dreaded his touch, not welcomed it. Not so with Al. Despite his size, Al had never made her feel physically inferior, never made her dread his presence or his touch.

Al's footsteps faded away from her until nothing was left but the steady drip of water somewhere nearby. She reached out a hand and ran her fingertips over the rough stone wall, the contact grounding her, tethering her to the world. She concentrated on breathing in and out, not allowing the darkness to press down on her.

After a lifetime, she heard Al's footsteps heading back towards her. She let out a long, steadying breath.

'This is it.' Al sounded excited. 'You'll need to stay by me as the going is quite rough but I think we can do it, even in this darkness.'

His large hand curled around hers again. She didn't like the way her body welcomed the contact but she wasn't strong enough to let go.

'How far did you manage to get?'

'Right to the end. It leads to a door, which has mostly rotted away. I was able to step through it and climb up into the courtyard. There are guards nearby, but if we are quiet we should be able to get around them without drawing attention to ourselves.'

Johanne's heart started to race. This was it. She was going to step into her enemy's stronghold. If they were caught, there was no going back. And yet, she only wanted to carry on. Her racing heart as exhilarated as it was terrified.

It seemed to take no time before they stepped through the rotten doorway.

Al stopped and turned to her. 'This is your last chance to go back. I won't think less of you if you do not want to go any further.'

'I want to keep going.'

He squeezed her hand. 'Then come on.' Together they carried on up and out of the tunnel, into the courtyard beyond.

Even though dusk had long since fallen, the courtyard was bustling with life; pools of light were dotted around the space. Alewyn pulled Johanne deeper into the shadows thrown by a nearby building. She came with him willingly, putting her trust in him.

'What is everyone doing? At Brae we are all eating by now.'

He smiled at the innocence of her words. 'Brae is special. You have created a place which feels warm and welcoming, even to a stranger. You should be proud of that. This place is more typical.' Realising what he'd said and how much he had revealed to her, he added, 'I would imagine.' It was a weak follow-up. If she'd been paying attention and not been worried about Brae, she would have questioned him intently about what he remembered from his past. He must be more careful, but the more time he spent with her, the more he felt his barriers crumbling. He wanted to talk to her, wanted to tell her about himself. It was madness. He was going to be the instigator of his own downfall and all because of an unwanted attraction to a woman who would never be his. Luckily for him, she was peering into the courtyard and was oblivious to his internal rambling.

'I was envisioning stockpiles of swords and longbows but I can't see anything at all.'

'I would imagine it takes an age to put together enough weaponry to mount a long and effective siege. Morcant is moving as quickly as he can, but that does not give him much time to prepare if he is going to strike soon. I guess that will be in our favour.' He didn't imagine or guess, he knew. He'd been on sufficient campaigns to know how much work went into successful preparations. If war with France escalated, then he would no doubt find himself in a battle or siege once more. It was his life and before coming to Brae he had not given it a second thought. Now he saw a different way, a castle that had turned away from violence, where it was not always about racing to the top and trampling on those beneath you to get to where you wanted to go. He liked it and would miss it once he returned to his normal existence.

'Should we try and see more?'

'Yes.' He should be concentrating on the mission at hand and not pondering his life's decisions. 'We'll move in this direction.' He indicated a path to his left.

They moved slowly. A noise sounded to their right and they froze but it was only a rat scuttling over some discarded scraps.

'My heart,' said Johanne, clutching her chest.

It was becoming natural to hold her in his arms, to pull her to him and offer her comfort. Too natural, in fact. But it seemed she liked it there because she snuggled against him, burying her head in his chest. He needed to let go, to stop this overwhelming feeling that he should protect her at all costs. He was getting too distracted from his mission, too caught up with her life. All his musings on Brae being the ideal place to live were ridiculous. He and Johanne did not belong together.

He dropped his arms. For a moment, she

stayed where she was. She realised he wasn't holding her on a soft inhale and backed away quickly. He cleared his throat, shifting on his feet.

Somehow, he had managed to make that awkward. No wonder he had yet to find a wife. Dear God. What was wrong with him? Why was he thinking about taking a wife now of all times? It was as if his brain could not think of more than one thing and that thing was Johanne and not the danger they were now in. She was an almighty distraction. The sooner he was out of her company, the better.

They started moving again. He didn't take her hand this time.

They rounded a corner and sucked in identical gasps of horror at the large weapon looming in front of them.

'A trebuchet,' whispered Johanne. 'Brae's walls cannot withstand a trebuchet.'

'They won't have to.' He turned on his heel and walked away. Now there was something he could do, something practical that would protect Brae.

Johanne could only stare in horror at the violent machine that towered over the skyline.

She had never seen such a weapon in real life, although she had heard stories. It was larger than she'd imagined. Its long arm hung innocently backwards, no hint of the damage it could wreak on thick castle walls. Brae's defences would not stand a chance. She should give in to Morcant, offer him Brae without bloodshed, before any of her people died. Perhaps they could come to an agreement, that Cineas would be Morcant's heir. He didn't have one of his own. Maybe she should marry him. It couldn't be any worse than being married to Badon and she had endured that. It would be worth it if nobody died.

'We need to leave.' Al reappeared at her side. 'Come. Let's move closer to the front gate. In the commotion we will be able to slip out unseen.'

'What commotion?' She looked about her, but nothing seemed out of the ordinary. Although... She sniffed. 'What's that smell?' An acrid scent was beginning to permeate the air.

'You can already smell it? I was hoping we'd have a little more time.'

'Al, you're not making sense.'

'I set fire to the trebuchet.'

She ground to a halt. 'What?'

'I set it on fire. Hopefully, it will not be spotted before much damage has been done. Preferably until it has burnt completely to the ground, but I doubt we will get that lucky, especially as you can already smell the burning wood.'

Her heart swelled, almost as if it were about to burst. 'I can't believe you risked yourself like that for me. If you had been caught...'

'We still might be caught if we don't get moving.'

The stench of burning wood now filled the air but still no one had called out a warning. Had Al really done it? Should they go back and check? But if he hadn't where was that smell coming from?

Laughter sounded nearby and Al pulled her deeper into the shadows. 'Johanne.'

'Hmm.' She couldn't understand it. How could people be laughing while the trebuchet burned? Why was no one running, shouting for help?

'Johanne.'

She could hear Al speaking, she could feel his hand on her arm, but he seemed so far away. What was happening to her? Behind her, she could hear him muttering curses.

'Johanne.' He whirled her round to face him. 'Johanne.' He spoke softer this time, brushing hair off her face with his fingertips. 'I know this is overwhelming, I know that it can seem confusing, but I need you to come back to me.'

What was he talking about? She was right here. She reached up and touched his face. His beard was soft against her skin.

'I need to get you back to the inn. Do you think you can walk?'

She frowned. Of course she could walk. She turned and stepped forward. The ground seemed to undulate beneath her and she stumbled.

Al cursed again. 'I've seen this happen before. I just didn't think… You seem so strong… I had forgotten you had never been in a situation like this before. Come here.'

Strong arms pulled her up and then she was slung over Al's shoulders as if she were a sack of hay. In the back of her mind, she knew she should protest. This was her mission. She should remain in charge. It was what she always did but she couldn't find it in herself to protest as her head bounced against Al's back.

Alewyn shifted Johanne on his shoulders. For a tall woman, she was incredibly light.

There was virtually nothing to her. He hadn't expected her to go to pieces. She'd seemed so strong but something inside her had snapped when she had seen the trebuchet. He understood that. She was not used to war and violence. Not in the same way he was. The fact that she was allowing him to carry her showed just how far she was from normal. She would never have given up control otherwise. But when she had started walking as if she'd had one too many ales, he realised she was not herself. When he'd spoken to her, he'd known just how far from reality she had gone.

When he'd seen it happen to young squires, he'd poured a bucket of cold water over them to bring them back to their senses. He didn't have that luxury here, although even if he had he couldn't have done that to her. She'd have frozen to death.

In the distance, he heard shouting. His small act of sabotage had been discovered. He only had to hope that enough time had passed for damage to really set in.

Footsteps ran past, the shouting getting louder.

He had to get them both out of here.

It would be a nightmare if they were caught.

His eyes had long since adjusted to the darkness, so he pressed back further towards the walls of the castle. In places, the going was difficult to navigate. Rubbish had been dumped behind wooden buildings and in places he had to clamber over it. All the while, Johanne said nothing.

The gate came into sight. Men were swarming around the exit like ants from a disturbed nest. There didn't seem to be anyone directing their actions, which would make it easier to slip through, but the sheer quantity of them might prove a problem.

He needed another distraction.

He gently lowered Johanne, keeping his arms around her until he was sure she was standing safely on her own. 'I'm going to get us out of here but I need you to concentrate. Do you think you can do that?'

She nodded. 'Yes. I am sorry about before. I am feeling better now.'

'You have nothing to apologise for. I should never have brought you into this situation.'

Her back straightened. 'You didn't have a choice in the matter. I would have brought myself if you had refused to accompany me.'

Her defensive side was back. Good. A docile

Johanne was not the person he was used to. It was far better to have her back to her normal contentious self.

'I'm going to cause a diversion. When the men from the gate move away, I want you to run.'

'What about you?'

'Don't worry about me. Just get away. Head back to the tavern. I will meet you there. If I don't turn up, then take Heled and ride to Brae as fast as you can manage.'

'But—'

'I know you don't like taking orders, Johanne, but this time, please listen to me. Out of the two of us, I am more expendable. Your people rely on you.'

For a long moment, he thought she would try to argue. In the end she only nodded and turned to face the gate.

'How will you get them away?'

'I'm not sure yet. I'm going to look around. Remember, run for the gate as soon as it is clear. Do not stop for anything.'

'I can remember that. I had a brief moment of panic but I did not become an idiot. You do not need to worry about me.'

She had closed down on him. She was showing him the front she put on for the rest of the world again. He should be glad. He wanted her hard, but he couldn't help the small part of him that was disappointed to see her acting like this in front of him once more.

'I will find you again.'

She nodded but didn't turn to face him.

Johanne stared at the main gate as she listened to Al's footsteps receding. She longed to call him back to her but he'd made it clear she needed to pull herself together.

Her knees shook.

Her heart raced.

She could barely breathe.

Badon's voice rang in her ears, reminding her of all the ways she'd failed him. If she didn't get out of here, everything he had said to her during the long days of her marriage would be true. She concentrated on breathing in and out slowly. Al had faith in her. He believed she would get out alive. She could do this.

Shouting sounded behind her but she didn't turn to look. The shouting grew louder and finally attracted the attention of the guards by the gate. They began to murmur amongst themselves and then a bang rang out through the night.

Almost as one, the men ran towards the noise and away from the gate. Heart in her mouth, Johanne raced towards the exit, keeping in the shadows until the last possible moment. Her breath caught in her throat as she stepped out of the complete darkness to make the final run to safety. Night had fallen, but if anyone looked her way they would undoubtedly spot her. She passed under the portcullis, half expecting someone to call out to her, but nobody did.

And then she was through the gateway and out in the open. She immediately stepped off the main path and began to run along the edge of it. She was almost back in the settlement when she stopped. It didn't feel right to continue without Al. He had risked his life for her and Brae and she had abandoned him.

She turned back to face the castle. Thick smoke was rising above the walls, obscuring the moon. To return to the tavern without Al would look suspicious, especially when something was obviously going on at the castle. She could hear the distant shouts coming from inside the defensive walls and even smell the thick, black smoke racing into the sky, blanketing out the stars. The townsfolk were bound to notice it soon.

Footsteps sounded on the path to her right; she shrank deeper into the shadows until she realised the large shadow was Al.

'Al,' she called.

'I thought I told… I thought you were going to return to the tavern.'

'I could hardly go in there without you. I might as well walk in there and tell everyone what we have been up to all evening.'

'I'm glad to see you're back to your normal argumentative self.'

'I don't argue. I…' Even in the darkness she couldn't miss the flash of his teeth as he grinned—infuriating man. 'Let's go.'

'Of course, mistress.'

His deferential tone didn't fool her for a minute. 'I preferred it when you called me Johanne.'

There was a pause. 'Johanne.' Her name on his lips, spoken that way, did strange things to her stomach. She squashed the odd sensation as she turned and made her way towards the door of the tavern.

The taproom had emptied out a bit during

their absence. A group of men still sat in one corner, their words mostly incoherent. A lone drinker stared down into his tankard and didn't look up as they stepped towards the innkeeper. He frowned at their approach.

'Did you get lost?'

Johanne glanced down at herself. She was caked in mud. 'Yes,' she said. 'Very lost.'

They stepped closer and Al leaned an arm across the top of the bar. He spoke quietly. 'Thank you for your directions earlier and for your words. We've been giving it a lot of thought and you are right. We should return to our home and not press on with our intended journey.'

'I think that's wise. Would you like a room for the night?'

Al hesitated and glanced down at her. For once she had nothing to say. What if she said yes? Her and Al in a room for the night, just the two of them with no responsibilities, nobody to know what they were doing. How would the scrape of his stubble feel against the softness of her cheek, the curve of her breast, on her hip? For so long, she had held on to her control; what would it be like to surrender it for an evening, to feel his strength as he took her? He would be focused, as he was with everything. For that brief time, she would be everything to him. She would not hold back. If it were for one night only, then she would give all that she was to him. She lifted her head and held his gaze, allowing her desire to show through. His eyes widened, his pupils blown. His lips parted and his gaze flickered over her body. And then he pulled himself upright, his expression becoming shuttered.

Al turned back to the innkeeper. 'No, thank you. We do not need a chamber for the night. We will start our return journey now.' Whatever he had seen in her gaze had not appealed to him. Her cheeks burned and she dipped her head. He didn't want her and that shouldn't matter, not with Brae's future on the line, but it did.

They saddled up their horses without speaking. Embarrassment tugged at her stomach making it ache. She'd thought he'd found her as attractive as she found him but that had been before. Now that he knew her better, something had obviously put him off.

She couldn't look at him as they led their horses out of stables and into the cold evening air. News that there was trouble up at the castle had spread and townsfolk were spilling out onto the streets to look at the smoke still billowing into the sky.

Al flung her up onto her saddle and vaulted up onto his horse. 'We'll walk our horses out of town and then we'll ride as fast as we can. It may take days for a connection to be made between the strangers at the tavern and the sabotage of the trebuchet, but we cannot risk it.'

Johanne nodded and followed him out of the stables at a sedate pace. Nobody spared them a second glance as they made their way out of the settlement, all eyes on the unfolding drama at Morcant's stronghold.

Once free of the town, they kicked their horses into swift motion and raced away from Ormond.

The temperature continued to drop as an icy wind whipped through the trees lining the route.

'I think I can hear water. We should stop and let the horses have a drink,' said Al when they were many leagues away from Ormond.

'You're right. I hadn't thought of Heled's comfort at all.' Guilt gnawed at her; she had asked her horse to go impossible lengths today and there were still several leagues to go until they reached Brae.

The river wasn't far from the path. She climbed down from Heled, grateful for a moment to stretch out her body. 'What do you think will happen when Morcant works out it was us who sabotaged his trebuchet?'

'What can he do? Unless he is completely lacking in wits, he will work out it was us fairly quickly. You are very distinctive.' Was distinctive good? Al was watching the horses and it was too dark to read his expression. 'He is planning a siege against you. You have got in the first hit.'

There it was again, the sense that he knew exactly what he was talking about, as if warfare was something he was familiar with, something that didn't shock him. There were things he'd said while they were inside the castle walls too. She should question him, but she didn't want to. Now was not the time to find out he was someone other than he was pretending to be. Not when she was so far from home. Not when she was beginning to imagine what it would feel like to have his mouth on hers, to press her body against his and to know what it would be like to be held in those strong arms. Not when he didn't feel the same way as her.

A twig snapped nearby and she jumped. Al's hand went to his waist, as it always did when he thought they were about to be attacked. He obviously wore a weapon in his normal life. Another twig crunched and Al pushed her behind him. She stepped close to his back; pushing herself onto her tiptoes she peered around his arm. 'What's happening?'

He didn't answer. His face was turned towards the spot from where the sound had come. She gently rested her fingers on his back, needing the comfort and something else she couldn't name. His muscles were tense, as if he were coiled for attack.

Leaves shuffled and she pressed herself closer.

She held her breath.

Al's body tightened.

And then relaxed. 'It's a fox.'

Her whole body sagged; she leaned against him, her legs unable to hold her upright any longer. He half turned and pulled her into his arms. His heart raced beneath her ear. She clung to him tightly. It was becoming a habit, this, to want to be held in his arms. She must not get used to the comfort he offered. He would be gone soon enough but she couldn't find it in herself to pull away—perhaps it was the exhaustion from the day, perhaps it was something else she did not wish to name; whatever it was, she was not going to step away.

'Johanne.' Hearing her name spoken so gruffly sent a shot of something powerful through her.

'Johanne,' he said again.

She turned her face up towards his. His jaw was tightly clenched, his eyes fixed on her. This time, there was no mistaking the fierce look in his eyes. She reached up and lightly touched his chin, the bristles of his beard soft against her fingers. His eyes shut and a long sigh brushed against her skin. She traced along the edge of his jaw, stopping when she touched his pulse, which pounded beneath her touch. She hadn't been wrong about his desire for her. It was as strong and as real as her own.

'Johanne.' His voice sounded pained. 'Johanne… I really…'

He dipped his head; his lips grazed over her forehead, and down over her cheeks to her jaw. His stubble brushed against her sensitive skin and she turned her mouth to his. He groaned softly as his lips skimmed against hers in the softest of touches, and again, light and teasing. It wasn't enough.

He began to lift his head but she followed him, pressing her mouth to his, unsure of what to do, only knowing that she did not want this moment to be over.

'Johanne,' he whispered against her mouth, her name sounding like a prayer. He did want this too; she was sure of it.

It was her turn to move her lips along the length of his jaw and down the column of his neck. Her heart swelled as he made a muffled grunt; the tight leash he had on his control slipped and he pulled her flush against his body. 'I want, more than anything...' His words faded as his fingers stole into her hair, cupping the back of her head and tilting her towards him. She licked her lips, craving his touch.

His mouth moved towards hers and then stopped. 'You are so beautiful, Johanne. I want to kiss you more than I want to breathe but I can't.' His fingers slipped from her hair, trailing down her arm, leaving her skin tingling with sensation even as his rejection hit her like a physical blow.

'What do you mean, you can't?' How could he be so tender and passionate one moment and then stop? Her body was screaming at her to carry on, to press her mouth to his and let the moment take them. How could he not feel it too?

'I'm sure it would be momentarily lovely but we would both regret it.' His voice had lost the passion that had burned in it only moments ago. He sounded practical, prosaic almost.

And what did he mean by they would both regret it? She stumbled backwards, needing to get away from him. He reached out to catch her but she moved away. 'I know why I might regret it.' His rejection had her spewing words she didn't mean. 'I made a promise to myself to avoid men for the rest of my life, but why would you regret it?'

He rubbed the back of his neck. 'I mean that I do not know who I am. It would be wrong to kiss you without knowing what sort of person I might be.'

'Oh.' He had a fair point but what sort of person could he be? He was kind and honourable. Her stomach dropped as a horrible thought occurred to her. 'Do you mean that you think you might be married?'

His response was immediate. 'Good God, no. I'm not married.'

'How do you know?'

There was a silence; her mind whirled. He had seemed so sure, not a shadow of a doubt in his mind, that there was no woman in his life. If he didn't remember who he was, how could he be so absolutely positive?

After what seemed like an eternity, he said, 'Whether I'm married or not just seems like something I would remember.'

'Hmm.' She wanted to question him, to press him on the details of his life that he remembered. The more this evening progressed, the more convinced she became that he knew something, if not all. It was in the way he had taken charge and how he had dealt with the trebuchet. She had stood frozen in horror at the sheer size of the killing machine. No coherent thoughts had permeated her mind. Even if they had, it would not have occurred to her to destroy it; she would have thought it impossible. Yet, he had not only known what to do, he had done it with a calmness that suggested he was used to such extraordinary occasions.

She shifted on her feet, the cold seeping through the soles of her boots. Should she question him or would that dredge up things she didn't want to know? Al had proved himself as a good man, a hardworking one who put her needs before his own. If he knew who he was, then he had his own motives for staying at Brae. Perhaps he was hiding from someone. Maybe he owed money or there was a jealous husband out there whom Al had cuckolded. No—she shook her head—Al would never do that.

'We need to get going.' She jumped at the sound of Al's voice; she had almost forgotten he was still standing in front of her, so close she could almost touch him.

'Yes. We should return to Brae before the sun rises. There is much to do tomorrow and we both need some rest.'

They climbed onto their horses in silence and made their way back to the path. Questions were building up inside her, threatening to come out but, for once, she managed to hold her tongue. The trees cleared and the path stretched before them; they kicked the horses into faster motion once more.

As the leagues passed she decided that all she needed to know about Al was that he was willing to help her and God knew she needed it. She may well be a coward in not pressing him further but if he helped her to protect Brae, then she would overlook his inconsistencies.

She had long since sworn to rely on no one but herself. That had held her in good stead for many years. She could use Al without getting too close. Tonight had been an aberration. She was exhausted and shocked by the day's events and she had weakened. It had felt good to be in someone's arms, to have someone next to her while her world fell apart, but she didn't need that support. She was strong. She had survived a brutal marriage, had managed to forge a place where she made her own destiny. She did not need Al in any other way than as someone who would help her protect Brae. She just had to stay out of his arms and stop any errant thoughts from now on.

Chapter Nine

Brae looked worse than Alewyn remembered and it had only been a day since he had last seen it. No wonder Morcant thought he could take it in a siege. It was a miracle the walls were still standing.

Dawn was approaching as their horses tiredly picked their way over the uneven road to its gates. His body ached after the gruelling ride of the last night and day and his mind hurt over what had happened between him and Johanne.

She hadn't spoken to him since they'd climbed back onto their horses. To nearly kiss her and then stop had been the worst kind of torture, even though he knew it was the right thing for him to do.

Whether he liked it or not, she was still a

suspect in the worst crime imaginable: treason. Even if everything was telling him she was innocent, kissing her when he hadn't proven it was beyond brainless. His body had urged him to claim her mouth, to make it clear she belonged to only him. Now, nearly half a night since he'd held her, his body was still raging with a need to make her his in every single way.

When he'd told her they would both regret it, he hadn't missed her wounded inhale or the way her shoulders had dropped. He should have chosen his words more carefully. The last thing he wanted to do was hurt her and yet her angry words had told him that he had managed to do that very well.

Besides, he hadn't given her the real reason she would regret it if they kissed. She would regret it because she wasn't kissing Al, the stranger who was helping her defend her castle. She was kissing Sir Alewyn, the knight sent to investigate her.

He couldn't truly give in to his desire for her when the lie stood between them, could not betray her like that. He could not give in to his desire at all. He could not offer her a marriage and she was not the sort of woman you tumbled and then walked away from. He was a man who was not sure where his future lay. She deserved someone who was secure in his world, who didn't doubt his own abilities. But he couldn't tell her that without revealing all and that was not possible. So, he would have to suffer his desire and make sure he didn't show her just how much he wanted her.

As they rode closer to the castle, Gemel appeared in front of the gate, his arms folded tightly across his chest.

'Where have you been?' he demanded as soon as they were in earshot. 'I was about to send out a search party. I imagined you were dead.' He was addressing Johanne, completely ignoring Alewyn. Alewyn understood. He would have been out of his mind with worry if he had been in Gemel's place.

'I told the guard I was taking Al out to see the extent of Brae's land and—'

'That excuse may have fooled the old guard but it doesn't make any sense to me. Brae is not big enough for it to take a whole day and night.'

'Everything is fine, Gemel. There is no need—'

'Johanne,' Alewyn cut in. 'There is no reason to hide where we have been. Gemel will need to know soon enough. We will not be able to do everything on our own.'

'But...' She turned to him and all his resolutions to keep away from her slipped away when he saw the anguish in her eyes. He gripped his reins tightly to keep himself from reaching out to her.

'You cannot hide it, Johanne.'

'No one will want to stay.' The words were whispered and his heart ached for her. She was so alone, fighting to keep her son's inheritance with no man to help protect her. Even if he was worthy enough to be that man, he couldn't be the one to give her the support she needed. His life was far away in Windsor, guarding the King and his interests.

'I'm sorry, Johanne, but he needs to be told. Everyone needs to be told.'

'Told what?' Gemel was watching their exchange intently.

'Do you want me to tell him while you rest?' He could do that for her, shoulder some of the burden.

She straightened in her saddle. 'No. I will do it. Then we will plan our counter-attack.'

She clicked Heled into motion and rode into

the castle without a backward glance. Anyone looking at her now would think she was
in control of her emotions. Now that Alewyn
was getting to know her better, he understood
the strength she needed to pretend all was well.
She was constantly putting on an act, constantly pretending to be someone she wasn't.
The walls she put around herself must be exhausting to maintain.

Johanne swayed on her feet but managed
not to sink to the floor and sleep where she
stood. She had not rested since she and Al had
arrived back at Brae at dawn. There had been
too much to do. Gemel had taken the news
that Morcant was planning a siege reasonably
well, considering. He and Al had immediately launched into creating a list of things that
needed doing urgently. Although she should
have taken charge of that, she had been content to let them get on with it.

She'd had the difficult task of letting everyone else know. She'd had to stand in front
of her people and tell them that Morcant was
going to make their lives a living hell. She'd
had to watch the mothers scoop up their children and hold them tightly. She had wanted,

then, to go to Cineas, to see him laugh and to listen to his childish chatter, but she hadn't. Instead, she had told her people that she would not force them to stay, that they were free to leave if they wanted. If it was still within her power, she would welcome them back afterwards.

Not one person had left.

By the afternoon, repairs on the castle walls had begun.

By the evening, a small but determined group of men had come up to Al and asked to be trained in combat.

Later, her women had come to her. They had sworn to do whatever it took to protect Brae and support their men in the coming battle. Her heart had swelled with hope and, since the first time she'd heard about the siege, she'd begun to believe that she could win.

It was only now that she was standing in the centre of the courtyard, looking around at everything that needed doing, that her fear came back to haunt her. In the stillness of the evening, she could imagine the broken bodies of her household and the walls of Brae in tatters and her heart bled at the images.

'You need to sleep, Johanne.' She jumped.

She hadn't realised Al was so close. 'You look nearly dead on your feet.'

She turned to him. 'How come you don't?' There were faint shadows beneath his eyes, but otherwise he looked as good as usual. 'You have had almost as little sleep as me.'

His lips tilted in his half-smile. 'Perhaps I am just better at hiding it. I can promise you that I am as exhausted as you are. I'm sure everyone will understand if we do not join them for the meal this evening.' When she didn't move, he slipped a hand underneath her elbow and gently tugged her towards her sleeping quarters.

Normally, she would protest at being led around. It was something that Badon had done. With her late husband, it had been a controlling gesture. She'd had no choice but to go where he directed. With Al, it was different. His touch was firm but gentle. She could move away from him if she really wanted to, but she found that she didn't. Her legs ached and she wasn't sure they could hold her up for much longer. That was why she welcomed his touch, nothing more.

'Tomorrow will be a long day,' he commented. 'But I am pleased with the progress made today.'

'What do you think of the men who want to train with you?'

His brief pause had her heart sinking. 'They are good men. I am sure several of them will be good fighters. Those that aren't will be useful backup. There will be plenty for everyone to do.'

They stepped inside. She expected him to stop at his chamber door but he began to propel her up the steps towards her own bedchamber.

'Which door is yours?' he asked when they stepped out into the narrow corridor.

'The one at the end.'

'You are directly above me.'

'Yes.' That fact had given her several sleepless nights already. She knew it was wrong to imagine her guest as he slept, but the images haunted her anyway. She'd only seen him lying on the mattress in the darkness of the night or when he'd been broken and bruised. It didn't matter. Her brain still conjured up images she would rather not see. When she closed her eyes she could picture his strong arms reaching out to pull her towards him. After that near kiss, the images would be much worse.

'I'll bid you goodnight then.'

'Yes. Goodnight. And thank you for everything you've done today.'

'Hmm.' He still hadn't let go of her arm. He was staring intently at her closed door, the expression on his face unreadable. She should step away from him. They had already agreed the near kiss between them had been a mistake but was he rethinking his decision? It didn't matter. She knew it would be a mistake, even if her body hadn't quite caught up with her brain. She tugged her arm from his. 'You are right, I must sleep.'

That seemed to snap him out of his trance. 'Of course. I will leave you.' He turned on his heel and almost ran for the stairs.

She watched him go, a strange heaviness in her stomach. It couldn't be regret that she hadn't invited him to her room. She didn't even enjoy the act that occurred between a man and a woman. Just because Al was not a brute did not mean that she would feel any differently. Yes, as his mouth had moved across her skin her whole body had come alive. And yes, the brief touch of his lips had brought her more joy than any moment during her marriage, but that did not mean anything. She was starved of affection after a lifetime without it. She had reacted as any woman would around a handsome man. It meant nothing.

She crossed over to her door and pushed it open. Once you gave men control over one aspect of you, they took control over everything. Al may be a better man than Badon but he was still a man.

Chapter Ten

〜〜〜

Al shrugged off his tunic and stripped down to his underclothes. Five days of working hard on mending Brae's castle walls and training the men who wanted to defend it should have worn him out completely. His body *did* ache with a bone-deep tiredness but his mind, *that* was full of images he was trying desperately to forget.

He climbed under the blankets and pulled them up to his chin. The room was cold but he did not want to waste time lighting the fire. He would warm up soon enough.

He closed his eyes and willed his body to sleep. He had no way of knowing if Johanne was in her own bed. She had left the Great Hall a while ago and not headed into the rooms she used to oversee the castle. She may well be with Cineas. Or she could be walking the battlements; in short, she could be anywhere, but these mundane, boring images were not the pictures his brain was conjuring up.

He imagined her in her bed. The same way he had every night since he found out she slept directly above him. Five nights of desperate longing, five nights of frustrated desire. He groaned as the images he tried so desperately to keep at bay assailed him once more. He pictured her, her coppery curls released from their braid and spread across her bedding, her blue eyes sparkling with laughter. In his fantasy, he was there with her. She was reaching up to him, slipping her hands around his shoulders and tugging him down. He would go willingly. He would not be able to fight his desire if he knew for certain that it was welcome. Her lips would taste delicious, her skin so soft to his touch.

He groaned as his body tightened. He was torturing himself.

It was wrong to desire someone from whom he was keeping such huge secrets. He knew that with every fibre of his being but that did not stop him thinking of her every moment of the day. He wanted her so badly, craved her as some men craved ale. Constantly pretending he was not affected by the way she moved or spoke or just existed was like a continual itch against his skin.

It didn't help that occasionally he thought he could see an answering flash of desire in her eyes. It added to the layer of torture to imagine that if he forgot his oath to the King's Knights, he could take her in his arms and she might not resist. That she might let him trace her long limbs with his fingers, learn what it felt like to touch the delicate skin at the base of her throat.

He groaned and rolled over, his erection digging into the mattress. He could take himself in hand but he knew from the last five nights that it made no difference. He still craved her even after his release.

What made it even worse was this was not all about desire for her body. *That* he knew he would get over given enough time. It was the desire for other things that worried him. He wanted to tease a smile out of her, to make her forget, even just for a minute, all the pressures that were piling down on her. He wanted to talk to her about the problems with Brae, to help her find solutions, so that Brae could go on to become a prosperous stronghold. He wanted to rub her shoulders until the tightness in her muscles relaxed and to join her when she talked to her son, to make them both laugh. In short, he was a fool.

Johanne was just another person he would eventually end up letting down. He knew nothing of land management or running a stronghold or raising a child. He knew nothing, really, other than how to fight. He could not be the man she needed in her life. He laughed, all trace of desire leaving him in a cold wave of realisation. She did not want a man in her life. She had said so many times. And those flashes of desire he'd thought he'd glimpsed in her eyes…they were always followed by a tightening of the barriers she wore around herself. She did not want him in any capacity.

He pushed himself to his feet. If he couldn't sleep, then he would be better served having a poke around while the rest of the castle's inhabitants slumbered. In the days he had spent at Brae, he was never alone for more than a few moments. By taking a stand against Morcant, Johanne was even more loved by her people than before, if that were possible, and not a single person would speak the slightest word against her. Not that he'd tried too hard. In his opinion, not only was Johanne not guilty of treason, neither was anyone in her castle.

He'd been so busy trying to make Brae defendable he'd almost forgotten the real reason he was here. Almost, but not quite. The impending threat of Benedictus's arrival, or even a messenger from him, was never far from his mind. If they arrived before he found the real traitor, then the threat to Johanne was far greater than Morcant's siege.

He pulled on his outer clothing and his thick cloak. His real clothes provided better protection against the biting wind than the garments he had borrowed. Winter had a severe grip on this part of the world and was not letting go easily. He was working so hard that he barely noticed during the day, but the nights were bitter.

The courtyard was empty; Brae's solitary guard was no doubt napping at his post. The men Alewyn was training would have to start taking shifts at guarding soon. They needed the practice at staying awake for long periods of time. They weren't ready yet; they were so inexperienced and were working so hard, they needed the nights to rest.

He had barely started with them, and the

amount of guidance he could give them in the short time he was here would not cover everything they needed to know to defend Brae from a siege. His heart ached when he thought of Thomas, the youngest of the recruits, who was barely out of childhood. He was so eager to please and so innocent.

Alewyn couldn't allow himself to think like this. Ultimately, his loyalty belonged to the King. To finish his mission was his priority. He would end up leaving the people of Brae to defend their home without him. He had to hope he would have done enough before he left. To imagine young Thomas lying defeated on the ground made him want to rage at the sky. Imagining Johanne in a similar state almost brought him to his knees.

He inhaled the frosty air. He must not think of this. If his mission failed, it wouldn't just be one of England's castles lying in ruin. It would be all of them. The country would be ruled by the French king, and Alewyn, and all his fellow knights, would be either dead or on the run. Failing in this mission was not an option.

He stepped deeper into the courtyard. A faint murmuring came from the Great Hall as the people who slept there settled down for the night. Lady Johanne hadn't asked him to join them, giving him a marked privileged above the rest of her household. He supposed she could hardly have her betrothed sleeping amongst her workers, but it was another thing, in a growing list of things, which made him aware of how much respect she was giving him and just how much he was lying to her.

He shook his head. He must forget that now and stop pondering on everything that was wrong. He needed to focus.

The people in the hall blocked his route to Johanne's antechamber. If there was evidence that either supported her innocence or condemned her, that was the most likely place for him to find it as that was where she conducted her business. Her ledger would be a good place to start. Perhaps he could access the rooms from a different angle. Brae was full of holes and only the largest of those had been patched up so far.

The main castle gate was closed and Alewyn didn't want to disturb the guard. He supposed he could pass his outing off as a training exercise but that excuse was weak at best. Besides, Johanne would likely find out and then he would be subject to her relentless barrage of questions. Lying to her even more would twist him up in further knots.

A section of the wall had crumbled slightly, not too far away from the entrance but enough distance that the solitary guard shouldn't notice his activities. It would not be easy for a man of his size to squeeze through, but he could probably do it without too much difficulty.

Habit had him sticking to the shadows as he moved around the courtyard, even though there was no one around to see what he was up to. The air was so quiet inside the castle walls. Alewyn could hear the faint roar of the sea as it swept across the pebbly beach below.

The gap in the wall was smaller than he remembered. His shoulders became wedged. Despite the seriousness of the situation, he couldn't help the bubble of amusement that ripped through him as he lay, his legs half dangling inside the castle and his head sticking out the other side.

If he'd thought waking up the guard to let him out was bad, how on earth would he explain this? He heaved and pushed, and sweat began to pool at the base of his spine. Just when he thought it wasn't going to be possible and that he would be discovered the following morning, probably as a pathetically frozen corpse, he popped out of the other side. He lay panting on the ground, staring up at the sky. That had very nearly been an inglorious end to his career.

He pushed himself to his knees. A few spots of icy rain hit his face. He glanced up; wisps of clouds scudded quickly across the sky. There was no moon to light up the surrounding area, although the stars provided some visibility. Alewyn stuck close to the castle battlements. An owl hooted above him; he flattened himself against the wall and then laughed at himself. If any of his enemies could see him now, they would be astonished to find him jumping at an animal's night-time call. Nearly getting stuck in the battlements had spooked him more than it should have done.

He walked on. There were no obvious entry points to the castle near where he guessed Johanne's antechamber to be. He sagged onto a fallen log and stared out at the inky blackness of the sea. The stars disappeared once more and he was plunged into an uneasy darkness. This place was nothing like Windsor, where there was always the noise of carts rattling over cobblestones or people talking as they went about their business. Here there was almost total silence. Only the rush of the sea as it hit the beach and wind rustling in the tops of the trees disturbed the night.

How long should he leave it until he returned to Windsor? He couldn't recall Benedictus giving him a date by which to complete his mission, but he knew his brother expected quick results for any of the assignments he handed out. Yet, if he returned without any definitive proof either way, then Benedictus would be disappointed. He shuddered at the thought.

Was it enough to say that deep down in his heart he didn't believe Lady Johanne capable of committing treason? That there was no way this sweet, courageous woman would do such a thing? Would Benedictus accept Alewyn's word? Was the bond between brothers strong enough? Years ago, Alewyn would have said yes but now... Benedictus had changed. He was becoming harder and more closed off as time passed and his role became more demanding. Benedictus was becoming more like their father, a man you avoided unless you absolutely had to speak with him.

It would be hard to convince Benedictus

without proof. He would believe Alewyn was being led by his cock and not his mind. If there was any way for Benedictus to meet Johanne that would be better, but they would only come across one another if Johanne was arrested for treason and by that point it would be too late. Benedictus would not see that Johanne was too naive to be a criminal mastermind, that she was too focused on keeping Brae safe for her son to spend time on anything else. His mind would already be made up about her.

In all their conversations, she seemed disinterested in France. There was no sense that she strongly opposed or supported the country.

And yet Alewyn knew there was a compelling reason why she may commit treason, why Benedictus would take some persuading and why he needed to stay at Brae until he had a counter-argument. Benedictus would see that she was a woman clinging to her property by the very tips of her fingers. At any moment, her authority could be challenged and she could lose everything. If she was desperate enough, Benedictus could argue that she had turned to England's enemy for financial support. Alewyn didn't believe that—Brae was not in a good enough state of repair for that to be the case—but was that enough? Could he risk her life based on his assumption alone? Would one Frenchman's confession that he'd come into England via Brae be enough to condemn her?

Alewyn stood. He would not find answers sitting on this log. He began to walk away but stopped as something caught his eye. Had he imagined it, or had there been a light down in the cove below?

He waited, barely daring to breathe. Yes. There it was again. A brief flash and then gone. Could that be a signal? And yes again. Longer this time but still only brief.

He began to move quickly. The track crunched underneath and he cringed; he was not built for stealth. He moved off the path, picking his way over roots he could vaguely make out in the darkness.

The path down to the beach was worn by thousands of previous footsteps. He'd not attempted it in daylight and had no doubt it would be difficult to negotiate in the dark. Voices approaching hit him before he began the descent. He dived into a bush as they came closer.

'...it was too windy. There was no way...'

'How will we know when…?'

He lost the thread when someone tapped him on the shoulder. He whirled around, throwing himself onto the body behind him.

'Ow,' a voice hissed in his ear.

He froze.

'Could you…?'

They both held still as footsteps sounded on the path nearby. When the sound faded away, the body beneath him wriggled.

'I'm sorry.' He rolled over.

'That's the second time you've squashed me.'

'I'm sorry,' he said again because what else could he say? This was a disaster.

'It's not your fault. I took you by surprise.'

It really was his damned fault. He was an utter fool.

'Have they gone?'

'I… I'm not sure.' This was awful. His whole mission was in tatters.

'Who were they?' demanded Johanne.

Denial was ridiculous and yet he couldn't stop himself clinging to the only possible way out of this mess. 'Who were who?

'The men coming up from the beach. Don't try and deny you were hiding from them. You wouldn't be in this bush if they were your friends. You also wouldn't be hiding in a bush if you weren't interested in what was going on. Tell me.' A slender finger prodded him in the arm.

'I…' Words failed him. This couldn't be happening. Why was she here? And of all people for him to stumble across…

'What were they doing on my beach?'

'I…' He sat upright. 'Why don't you tell me who they were and why you are hiding in this bush?' His stomach dropped. If she'd planned to meet them, then that meant…

'Oh, no. I am not telling you one more thing about anything. Not until you answer some of my questions.'

'I'm always answering your questions,' Alewyn growled, fury finally making an appearance. There he'd been, about to make a breakthrough in his mission, and instead he'd compromised it in the worst way imaginable. He wanted to ram his fist into something.

Johanne shifted beside him. 'I think we should return to the castle and talk about this in front of a fire. My hands are so cold I can no longer feel the ends of my fingers.'

Alewyn thought about protesting. He should

go after the men, but they'd probably be long gone. He'd have to have this discussion with Johanne at some point; he had to know why she was skulking about at night while strange men walked across Brae's beach. Once that was done, he could work out how to find those men.

He crawled out of the bush, brambles scraping the backs of his hands. He pulled them to one side as he helped Johanne through.

They didn't speak as they made their way back to the castle. Alewyn tried to think of a reason to explain to Johanne why he had been creeping through the dark but his mind stayed persistently blank.

Johanne let Al lead the way. She could argue that she wanted to know which way he'd exited the castle, because if a man the size of him could fit through, then Morcant was going to have no trouble. It would not be the truth. She enjoyed watching him walk; the way his muscular body powered through a space was fast becoming her favourite thing to observe. She'd become an expert in the way he moved; she had a hard time doing anything else other than look at him when he was around.

This evening, the strength of his stride was dimmed. The energy was still there but his head was bent as if it were too heavy and there was something in the slump of his shoulders that suggested he was deeply unhappy. It made her heart ache and yet she knew she must harden it against him. Whatever his reason for being at Brae, it was not as clear-cut as he had led her to believe. He had definitely been watching those men, men who were clearly up to no good within Brae's territory.

She tilted her head up to the sky, whispering prayers on the wind, prayers that Al would prove to be good and true even as she knew it was too late to change who he was. She did not want him to be involved in something unlawful or to have done something faithless. She wanted him to be as decent as he appeared. His actions since he had arrived at Brae had begun to restore her belief that some men were decent; she did not want him to rip that faith to shreds right now.

He moved along the outer wall of the castle until he reached the gap in the stonework, a gap of which she was already aware but which she hadn't thought that big. 'You can't possibly fit through there.'

She was rewarded with his half-smile, the one that always did strange things to her stomach. Tonight was no exception, despite all her worries about who he truly was.

'It was a bit tight coming through. Why don't you go first? That way, if I get stuck, then at least one of us will get to their bed tonight.'

She laughed but did as he suggested. The wind was bitter tonight and she wanted to get inside as soon as possible.

'I'm through,' she called when she'd reached the other side. Her heart stopped for a moment when it looked as if he wasn't following her, when she thought he may have run off to avoid speaking to her, but it soon became clear he was slow because of the size of the gap. In the darkness, it was hard to make him out and she only knew he had started to follow her by his grunting. Gradually the thick strands of his dark hair became visible. She bit her lip as laughter gurgled up inside her. His head came through and then his shoulders. There was no movement for a moment. She stepped forward to help him, although she had no idea how she would do that—pull sections of the wall down, she supposed. Before she could reach him, he fell through the last bit, landing by her feet like a beached dogfish. She couldn't stop the laugh that burst out of her.

He grinned sheepishly up at her and her heart began to race. When you looked past his intimidating size, he was adorable. The combination of strength and vulnerability was completely disarming. Women must fall at his feet. Jealousy, sharp and unexpected, curled in her stomach at the thought and she turned away lest her thoughts show on her face. She must not think like that. He was not hers to get possessive about. She didn't *want* to be possessive about him; he would go, possibly sooner rather than later. And *that* was what she wanted. She wanted to be alone, to shape her own destiny without the interference of another man in her life.

Besides, he was hiding something from her, and until she knew what it was, she could not afford to even think of him as a friend, despite everything he had done for her.

She heard him pull himself upright and when she turned back to him she made sure all humour had gone from her face. He looked at her and his smile slowly died. 'We need to talk.'

He nodded slowly. 'Aye.'

She began to walk, hoping he'd follow but knowing there was nothing she could do about it if he decided he didn't want to. She heard his footsteps and released the breath she was holding.

'Where are we going?' he asked.

'To my bedchamber.'

'Where you sleep?'

'Yes.'

He ground to a stop. 'Do you think that is wise?'

No. It probably wasn't. He was a man she had spent so much time thinking about, wondering whether the fleeting kiss they had shared would be so much better if it were deepened. A room where there was only the two of them and her bed was not wise, but there wasn't any other option. To get to her antechamber, the place where she conducted her business, would mean walking through the Great Hall and disturbing all those who slept there. 'It is the safest place we can talk undisturbed.'

'But we will be there alone, together.'

'I trust you.' At least, she did trust him with her body. There had been that time when he could have kissed her and he hadn't and the time at the inn when she was sure the desire she had for him was written all over her face. He could have had her then, if he'd wanted, but he hadn't. She was sure he was honourable about that, if nothing else, but then perhaps she was deluding herself. 'Am I wrong to do so?'

He let out a long sigh. 'I'll not take advantage of your body. You can put your faith in me with that.'

And in his answer, he gave away much. He had been hiding something from her, something that meant she shouldn't trust him completely. She'd suspected as much and yet the truth hurt her chest, as if someone had stabbed a knife right through her heart. She had believed in him more than she had anyone else in years, if not ever. She had relied on him to give her his help; she was still relying on him. Everyone in Brae had complete faith that he was exactly who he said he was and that he would guide them through the nightmare of Morcant's siege. And now... 'You'd better not be in league with Morcant or it will not matter how much smaller than you I am, I will still kill you.'

He smiled briefly. 'I am not in league with Morcant. That doesn't mean you might not want to kill me.' He shrugged. 'We had better get this over with.'

He walked past her, towards their sleeping quarters. He paused outside the door to his chamber but she swept past him and climbed the stairs to her own. They would do this on her terms.

Her knees began to shake as she heard his heavy tread on the steps behind her, but whether that was due to worry about what she was about to find out or for some other reason, she wasn't sure. She had not had a man in her chamber since Badon's death. Had not wanted anyone coming into the space that was her own private domain. Even her servant, Mary, was only allowed in for short periods to clean the room. It was her sanctuary.

She stepped into the room and paused. She still had time to turn around, to take this conversation elsewhere, but he came in behind her and the moment passed.

To stall for time, she made her way over to the fireplace. The flames were burning low in the grate. She threw another log on and poked about in the embers. She did not know how to begin. She almost didn't want to know. She took a deep breath and turned. Al had settled in the chair by her dressing table, his bulk making it look impossibly spindly. She was glad he hadn't chosen her bed to sit on. She didn't think she would be able to get that image from her mind once he had gone.

She settled on the edge of her mattress and found that she didn't know what to do with her hands. Resting on the bed seemed suggestive somehow. She settled on clasping them together and placing them on her lap, rather like a virgin on her wedding night.

'I want you to tell me everything.' Her request would have been more powerful if her voice wasn't shaking.

His smile was sad. 'Lady Johanne, you are putting me in a very difficult position.'

'I thought we agreed on Johanne.' Her voice was small and she hated it.

'Why were you out there this evening?'

'I thought I was asking the questions.'

'Not this time.' There was no threat in his voice but his gaze was firm and steady. She would answer his question if it meant getting to his answers quicker.

'I've been finding it difficult to sleep these last few nights. I find watching the tide soothing. I was on my way down to the beach when

I heard those men heading down to it. I thought they might be something to do with Morcant and so I stayed to watch. Not that much later, you landed on me.'

He rubbed his face before resting his arm on the table. 'Lady Johanne, what do you think about the war between France and England?'

'Why do you want to know about that?'

'It's important.'

She shrugged. 'I think the war is pointless. I think men will die for a piece of land that most English men or women will never see and will not profit from. The French are entitled to that land, in my opinion. I know that is not a popular point of view.'

His gaze dropped to the floor near her feet. He inhaled deeply and looked back up, his gaze locking on hers. She wiped her hands on her skirt; there was no need for her to be nervous and yet the look in his eyes was causing her heart to race unpleasantly. This was not the Al she recognised.

'Are you bringing Frenchmen into the country so that they can attack the King from within?'

All the air rushed out of her lungs. She stood and stepped towards him, but the room spun and she stumbled. Before she hit the ground, he caught her around the waist. 'Easy, Johanne. Take a deep breath.'

He tugged her back to the bed and sat next to her, rubbing her back in gentle circles, but the gesture was not reassuring. She stood and his hand dropped onto the mattress.

'Is that what you think of me? That I would do that? Is that why you are here? Oh, my goodness, Gemel was right. You have been lying to me the whole time. Am I going to be…?' She clutched her throat, unable to swallow at the thought of a noose tightening around it. 'Cineas…' she whispered. 'What will become of him?'

'Johanne.' She stopped and looked down at Al, who was regarding her calmly. 'Answer the question.'

She straightened. 'I would never do such a thing. I cannot believe that for one small moment, you would think me capable of such treachery.'

He nodded. 'I see.'

'That is why you are here. To find out if I am guilty of treason.' It seemed obvious now. How could she have been so foolish? A man like him had just happened to stumble across

Brae and she had taken it as good fortune. How gullible she had been.

'Yes. That is why I am here.'

'You are an agent of the King?'

'Yes. I am one of the King's Knights.'

Her knees weakened and she sank onto the mattress next to him. 'The King's Knights,' she repeated. Her head swirled. It was too much to take in. The King's Knights were legendary. There were only four of them, as far as she was aware, but they ruled the country with iron precision. Nobody, *nobody*, defied them unless they were truly brainless and wanted to end up dead or rotting in some dungeon. And she had one of them in her castle, in her bedchamber, no less. She had willingly allowed him into her life and had shared things she had told no one. Badon had been correct when he had told her she was not fit to rule Brae. She was an utter fool.

'Which of the King's Knights are you?' Her voice came out as a whisper.

'I wasn't lying when I said I was Sir Alewyn. My family name is Monceaux.'

She closed her eyes. It got worse. The Monceaux family were one of the most powerful dynasties in the whole country. If they thought she was guilty of treason… Cineas would be guilty by association. The Monceaux family could absorb Brae into their territories and no one would take up arms to prevent it.

'Are you here to arrest me?' she whispered. 'I swear to you I have done nothing wrong. But I cannot prove it.'

His hand twitched, as if he were about to hold hers, but it remained next to him. Even though he was her accuser, she missed his re-assuring touch. She realised she had become used to his light touches and she cursed her-self anew for being such a fool.

'For now,' he said. 'Please answer the ques-tion plainly—are you bringing Frenchmen into the country so that they can attack the King from within?'

'No.' She waited a beat. 'But wouldn't I say that anyway? I mean—'

'Johanne. Stop talking.'

'I would never—'

'Johanne.'

'I…' This couldn't be happening. She stood and walked towards the centre of the cham-ber. She'd thought life would be far simpler after Badon's death, but it had only become harder. At least when he was around, he made her decisions for her. And yes, she had hated that, hated having so little control over her life, but now that she had the authority, she had made a mess of it. A decision she had made or something she had overlooked in the past had somehow led her to this. A situation where she could be hanged for treason. A crime she would never dream of committing.

She would not give up though, not without a fight. She glanced back at Al. Fine, so she couldn't fight Al physically, but she would find a way to defeat him in this. She would prove her innocence; she just had to get him to allow her the time to do it.

'Johanne.' She was scaring him a little. First there had been the rambling and now there was the fierce scowling with some agitated pacing. He'd seen her shocked and confused before and he didn't want to deal with that again. She was a warrior, this woman, and he preferred her that way. Seeing her defeated hurt his heart in a way he did not want to analyse.

'Johanne.'

This final call of her name had the desired effect. She advanced towards him, her eyes blazing with fury. Alewyn forced himself to remain straight-faced. She would not appreciate him laughing but there was something about her expression which made his heart sing. Her eyes were captivating as they flashed with fury. He loved that she had complete belief in her ability to destroy him, despite the difference in their respective sizes. His pulse thudded erratically; she was magnificent.

'You have lied to me. Was everything…?' She waved her hand around as if to encompass all that had passed between them. Even the things that they had agreed should never happen again.

'Not everything.'

Her eyes flashed again. 'Which parts then?'

'Everything to do with Morcant, helping you plan against the siege. That has all been real.'

She sucked in a breath. 'Why were you lying on that path the day Gemel and I found you?'

'That I still don't know. I get flashes sometimes, during the night. Like I told you on that first day. Now there is more detail. There's a storm and I'm being thrown from my horse; she's screaming.' He shuddered. He had to hope that Ffleur was alive. She had been with him a long time. 'I think there are men there. My fist connects with someone and there is shouting and the sound of footsteps running but I don't understand how I came to be unconscious. It's all still a blur... I can't believe that I lost a fight. I haven't lost one in years, certainly not since I gained this height.' He tried smiling but she did not look impressed. He tried a different direction. 'The more I've come to know you, the more convinced I am that you are not involved in the plot.' Her shoulders relaxed a bit, but she continued to glare at him.

'Why did you think that I was involved in treason in the first place? Brae is in the middle of nowhere and is of no importance.'

'I...' He leaned forward, resting his arms on his knees. 'I don't think you are but...' He rubbed a hand over his face. 'The fact is, Johanne, there have been several Frenchmen caught near Windsor. They have been interrogated and revealed that they are coming into England via the south coast. One of them named Brae as their point of entry. That was enough to warrant an investigation into you.'

Her mouth opened and closed. She turned and walked around the room, her fingers running over a tapestry that covered the whole of the far wall.

He waited a moment for her to speak but

when she didn't, he carried on. 'I was sent here by Sir Benedictus. He is the leader of the King's Knights and my older brother. He wanted me to discover the truth before sending in the King's army. We didn't want to get the wrong person and reveal to the guilty party that we were on to them.' Even though he shouldn't be telling her any of this, he began to feel lighter than he had in weeks. It was good to have the truth between them. It felt right.

'Why do you think I'm not guilty?'

He stood too. 'I don't think you would put Brae at risk by committing treason.'

She nodded and the fight visibly drained out of her. Alewyn forced himself to stand still, refusing to let himself go to her, to touch her, to pull her into his arms to offer her comfort. Yesterday, his support may have been welcome but now…he was probably the last person she wanted anywhere near her.

She wrapped her arms around herself, looking younger and more vulnerable than he'd ever seen her. 'If it's not me, then who is it?'

'I don't know but I'm trying to find out.' Never had he felt more useless. 'I believe this is the way to prove your innocence. Sir Benedictus is unlikely to accept just my word.' And this was his guiding principle for this whole mission. Not just to discover the truth but to prove his own worth, that he was as capable as his brother knights. 'If I tell him that my only evidence is that I don't believe you guilty, he will think I have been beguiled by your beauty and will send someone else to—'

'Oh...'

He only realised what he had said, what he had revealed, when he noticed the pink spreading across her cheeks. His own skin heated in response. 'I mean, you're obviously a very beautiful woman but that's not why I think you are innocent.' His skin was beginning to burn now. 'I mean, I'm not the greatest spy. My strengths lie in my physical abilities. I can hit people very hard. It's not the most useful of skills; other people are better placed to solve mysteries. But they were elsewhere and so there was only me.' He was pacing now, desperate to stop talking but seeming unable to do so.

'I want to help.'

Her words stopped him in his tracks. 'What?'

'I want to help clear my name.'

She'd come back to the centre of the room and was standing directly in front of him. If he reached out an arm, he could pull her to him. The temptation was almost overwhelming. He hadn't held her since the night they'd rushed back from Morcant's stronghold. The night he'd nearly given in to his desire to kiss her. It was only the knowledge that he was lying to her that had held him back that night. He did not want to be the sort of man who lied but took what he wanted anyway. Now the truth lay between them and yet it did not make it better. He could no more hold her now than he had been able to before.

'I understand why you want to help but you must concentrate on building Brae's defences. I will not let Benedictus arrest you.' How he would do that, he wasn't sure yet, but he would make it so that it was true even if he had to fight his brother. He paused. Had it really come to that? He glanced at Johanne; her coppery curls glinted in the candlelight. Yes, it had. If Benedictus failed to listen to reason, then Alewyn would fight him for Johanne's freedom. He would fight the King's army if that was what it would take to keep Johanne from rotting in one of Edward's dungeons. He rubbed his chest. It was tight. What was happening to him? To fight his brother would be to risk everything he had worked for…but how could he not?

She nodded, unaware of the seismic shift going on inside him. 'I will continue to prepare Brae for the siege but helping you must also be a priority. If I defend Brae only to be subsequently executed for treason, Brae will most likely fall into Morcant's hands and all my effort will have been in vain.'

As she was speaking, she had stepped even closer towards him. He wondered if she realised how close they were now. Whether she wanted the comfort he was so keen to give her. He reached out and lightly touched the back of her hand. She turned her palm to face his and their fingers laced. For a moment, he thought she might step towards him so that he could take her in his arms, but he sensed her barriers being put back into place and she stepped away, dropping his hand and returning to her place on the edge of her mattress. She crossed her arms under her chest, giving every signal he was not to join her on the bed.

He settled back into the chair and watched her face. He wondered if she was aware of how her expression changed as she thought. She would not make a good courtier. She would not be able to scheme and lie in a place that was rife with back-stabbing plots. Right now, she was coming to some sort of conclusion, a positive one if he had to guess.

'It has to be Morcant.' She was looking brighter now, sitting upright, her eyes shining. 'That's why he's so keen to get hold of Brae. He would have ease of access to the coast and...' She trailed off.

'He has access to his own part of the coast though, doesn't he?' Alewyn had considered Morcant before and dismissed him for various reasons, although he would have loved to be proved wrong. His guilt would solve two problems. 'In that direction, he is closer to France than you are here.'

'Yes, but...' He hated to see the light in her eyes dimming. 'It still makes sense for it to be him. Why else would he want to marry me so badly?'

'Because he's greedy and by making Brae part of his territory he would command a large swathe of the south coast. Also, it might be...' He trailed off, his skin burning once more. She had made it very clear she wasn't interested in him so there was no need for him to embarrass himself by mentioning that Morcant might want to marry her so he could bed her whenever he wanted.

His own body stirred as he imagined a lifetime with her in his bed. He gritted his teeth; now was definitely not the time.

'It might be…?' She prompted.

'Forget it.' He spoke more harshly than he meant to and winced as she recoiled.

A log fell in the grate, sparks hissing into the room. They both turned and watched the flames for a moment.

'It's possible it's Yonescu.'

She turned to him sharply. 'What? No. It can't be him.'

He shifted in the chair. 'Why not?'

'Because he's my ally. He's always supported me, right from the beginning.'

Alewyn had picked Yonescu's name out of the air, more to break the ice between them than because he had given it any serious thought. The more he thought about it now though, the more it seemed like it could be a possibility. 'Don't dismiss my reasoning until you have heard me out.'

She snorted and crossed her legs. 'Go on.'

He rubbed his forehead. He would like to go, to give her time to relax, because he could say anything to her now and she wasn't in the mood to hear it. 'Yonescu's stronghold is not on the sea.' She nodded. He took that as a positive sign. 'And there was that attack on you.'

'That was Morcant.'

'One person mentioned Morcant. That was odd, don't you think?' She didn't nod her head but she appeared to be listening. 'Remember when we entered Morcant's castle, we did everything in our power to remain undetected. Surely, your attackers would have done the same. If they were truly working for Morcant, they would have kept his name hidden. That someone mentioned it stands out to me.'

She unfolded her arms. 'Go on.'

'How would Morcant have even known you were going to be in that part of the country?'

She opened her mouth to answer and then closed it again.

'He wouldn't but Yonescu would. It was Yonescu who told you about the stonemason. It was Yonescu who set up the meeting and it was Yonescu who gave you the meeting place.' Alewyn was really starting to believe his own theory now. His only question was why he hadn't thought about it in the first place.

'That is all true, but if Yonescu has a spy

in Morcant's household, the same is probably true of the reverse.'

Alewyn pondered this. 'Yes, but if he does have a spy at Yonescu's stronghold, then it was even more important for Morcant's name not to be mentioned during the attack on you. Think about it, Yonescu was the person who came to you with the news that Morcant was going to lay siege to Brae.'

'Which is true, and which is helpful to me because now I have time to plan my counter-attack.'

'True. But if a siege is going on here for months, both you and Morcant are only pay-ing attention to one another, meaning neither of you are watching your coastline. If we were able to investigate, we might find that Yonescu has been in talks with Morcant as well as you. I am willing to bet everything I own that Mor-cant thinks Yonescu is his ally.'

Johanne stood and made her way over to the fireplace. She selected a log from a basket by the fire and threw it into the grate. 'What could he have said to Morcant?'

'I don't know for sure, but I would guess he has suggested to Morcant that he move soon on Brae. My arrival on the scene may have prompted him. You are too busy with your current duties to notice goings-on down on the shoreline but with a husband your duties would be halved. You or I might have time to meander down to the beach where we might find something.'

She poked at the flames. 'Unless we are involved in a protracted siege.'

'Exactly.'

'If Yonescu hadn't warned me, then I would not have begun preparing. Brae would be completely unprotected and I would have fallen to Morcant within the first week, but now...'

'Now you have had time to prepare, the siege will go on for some time.'

She sank onto the rushes in front of the fire. 'This is a lot to take in.'

'Yes.'

'And, for now, it is only a theory.'

'It is. But it is plausible.'

She pulled her knees up to her chest. 'It is. Do you know, I didn't really like Yonescu when I was married to Badon? I thought he was insincere. It was only after Badon's death that I changed my mind. I thought my initial feelings were because my fear of Badon coloured everything around me. I should have trusted my instincts.'

'We must keep in mind that Yonescu might not be guilty. We must find proof first. If it turns out that he is behind the treasonous plot, you must not be too hard on yourself. Yonescu took advantage of you when you were vulnerable.'

Her head shot up at that and their eyes met. The message in her gaze was clear—how was that any different from what he had done?

He dropped his gaze and studied his hands. 'I've been on your side since I arrived, even if it doesn't seem like it.'

She didn't comment and his heart ached. He'd done everything right—not betrayed his oath and done everything in his power to make sure Brae was protected from Morcant—and yet he had still managed to hurt her.

Her opinion of him shouldn't matter. He would be gone from her life in a matter of weeks and it was unlikely he would ever see her again. He would probably be in France fighting for the King before the end of next year and she would stay in Brae, keeping suitors at bay and making sure the settlement prospered. And yet, it did matter. He wanted her to think well of him and there was nothing he could say to himself that would stop that desire.

Johanne watched a myriad of emotions cross Al's face, none of them she could read or understand. Al. That wasn't quite his name, only the part of it he had shared with her. Yet, even knowing that, she couldn't think of him as Sir Alewyn.

The firelight flickered, casting shadows over his face, a face that was so familiar to her now. He had been her friend and ally. She had come to think of him as the only person she had ever truly known and now it had all been revealed as a lie. He was Sir Alewyn, a man so much higher up in society's order than her that he might as well live on the moon. He was a confidant of the King and a Monceaux; he was one of the men leading the country whereas she was just trying to survive to the next day. Any growing connection between them had been in her imagination. The pain she was feeling in her chest was pointless. Two months ago, she hadn't even met him and within the month he would probably be gone for ever. His lies shouldn't matter.

She needed to focus on her original plan, the one she had hatched when she had found him on the path. She would use him to help her fix Brae's problems and then let him go. She could not keep him even if she wanted to. He belonged to the King, not her. 'How do we find out if Yonescu is guilty and prove that I am not?'

He looked up at her once more. 'That is where I am stuck.'

He sounded so bleak that her heart ached. She willed her features to remain blank. She did not want him to know that she felt anything for him, not even sympathy. Her pride would feel better that way. 'The men were talking about full moons and wind when I overheard them.'

'How long is it until the next full moon?'

'Tonight was a new moon. So, there won't be a full moon for around two weeks.'

He nodded. 'It makes sense that they would want to conduct their activities under the darkness of a new moon. They'll not want to smuggle anyone in with a full moon lighting up the night's sky. Tonight was windy. Perhaps it was too difficult to land a boat. Maybe they will try again tomorrow.' He nodded again. 'I will lie in wait and watch.'

'*We* will lie in wait and watch.'

He regarded her steadily for a moment. She held his gaze. She would not back down on this.

He broke first. 'It is too dangerous.'

'More dangerous than infiltrating an enemy's castle?'

'No, but—'

'More dangerous than a siege?'

'No, but—'

'More dangerous than living with an unpredictable, violent man?'

Al stilled. 'Badon was violent towards you?'

'Not often, but I could not always predict his mood. There is no need to look quite so murderous. It's not uncommon for a husband to hit his wife.'

His fists clenched. 'It should never happen.'

'No, well, I am glad to see that we agree on that. It is irrelevant for my future. I do not intend to marry again. My point is, I have faced danger before and lived. Brae is my castle and I should be the one to oversee its defence.'

'It would not harm you to rely on others sometimes.'

'When I find someone I trust implicitly, then I will do so.'

He reared back as if she had punched him and her heart twisted. 'I suppose I deserve that,' he said quietly. 'Very well. Tomorrow we shall plan our next move. Now, we both need to get some rest.'

He stood and made his way towards her chamber door. Part of her wanted to stop him, to tell him that she had always trusted him, but she held her tongue. She had naively believed everything he had told her, and even though he was proving to be a good man, it did not negate the fact that he had lied to her. She had been hardening her soul ever since her marriage to Badon, and she would continue to do so until she was no longer a naive and gullible fool. Only then would she be a worthy leader of Brae.

The door closed softly behind him without another word spoken between them.

Chapter Eleven

Johanne knocked gently on Al's door. It swung open immediately, suggesting he had been waiting directly on the other side. His body filled the entire frame and she was hit once again with the urge to run her hands over his muscled arms. She inhaled a shaky breath. Today had crawled by as she waited for the night to come. Now it was here, her knees were trembling. Tonight could mean the difference between life and death for her and that wasn't even at the forefront of her mind. She would be spending time alone with Al, potentially most of the night. The first time since the whole truth was between them. What would they talk about?

He cleared his throat. Heat swept over her as she realised she was standing staring at him.

She quickly stepped to one side to let him out. His sleeve brushed her arm and she shivered as she followed him.

'It's a shame the hole in the wall was blocked up today. I was looking forward to seeing you squeeze through it again,' she said as they strode into the courtyard.

His lips curved in her favourite half-smile and she turned away, not wanting to be charmed by him. 'I'm sure I can humiliate myself in some way to keep you amused.'

She grinned but made sure to keep her face turned away from him. She didn't want him to think he was forgiven for lying to her even though her heart had already started to soften. Now that she'd had time to think, she could see that he'd had no choice but to lie to her.

He was a spy and she was under suspicion for treason. If he had told her the truth, he would have betrayed the King. A knight did not get to his position in life without complete loyalty to the monarch. It was a testament to the strength of Al's character that he had stuck to his mission while also helping her prepare Brae's defences. He hadn't had to help. He could have walked away from her as soon as he'd decided she wasn't guilty and left her to cope with Morcant's attack all by herself. Even though she knew all this and understood, it didn't stop her being hurt by his lie.

'I had the guard wait up for us. I told him it was for a training exercise,' she told him.

He nodded. 'Good. From tomorrow we need to start putting the new guards on rotation. It shouldn't just be the one person who has experience of guarding at night. I would suggest having three who—'

'Out of the volunteers we've had, how many of them do you think would be able to stay up for a whole night? Saxon would be asleep almost straight away. And John... I don't think John would make it much longer.' She swallowed down a bubble of laughter as she imagined the oldest member of her household deeply asleep as Morcant's men approached.

Her ragtag group of Brae's protectors was made up of the men who weren't equipped to fight. They were either too old or too young. She'd given everyone the option to participate or not and there hadn't been a single person who hadn't volunteered to do something. Brae had been a hive of activity ever since she and Al had returned from Morcant's stronghold with their news of an impending siege.

'It's surprised me,' she said, voicing her thoughts out loud.

'What has?'

'I thought Brae would rapidly become deserted when we broke the news about Morcant's siege but everyone has rallied round.'

'That is because of you.'

'I haven't forced anyone!'

That knee-weakening half-smile again. 'I didn't mean that. It's because of the home you have created at Brae. People have stayed out of loyalty to you.'

She twisted her fingers together. 'I'm not sure I want that either. I don't want to be the reason people die.'

'You won't be. If there are any fatalities, Morcant will be responsible.'

Johanne's stomach turned. There was no way around it—some of her people would die as they defended Brae. In the dark hours of the night, she'd considered marrying Morcant. Her life for her people's safety did not sound so bad. The morning had brought a different reflection. Her marriage would stop any initial bloodshed. The threat of a siege would be over but life under Morcant's rule would begin. His bloodthirstiness was legendary. Life under Morcant would be no better for her than it would be for the inhabitants of Brae. Her people would die anyway.

She shuddered and Al glanced down at her. She shook her head as they reached the castle's gate and passed through unhindered. She did not want to talk about it now. She would deal with one problem at a time. 'Where did you build the shelter?'

Al had been out earlier and found somewhere for them to remain unseen while they waited to see if the men turned up again.

'Down here.' He steered her away from the main path down to the beach. Brambles pricked at her legs as she followed him through the spiky undergrowth.

'It's steep here. Let me…' He crouched and jumped down a small ledge. He turned and held out a hand to help her down.

She hesitated. They had touched last night for the first time in days. He had lightly brushed the back of her hand and, in a moment of weakness, she had laced her fingers with his. His skin had been warm and comforting but she had just found out he had lied to her and she had been angry with him. She had pulled away, relishing the flash of hurt she had seen on his face. But now, she was calmer.

He held his hand steady as she stared at it. Slowly, she reached across the space and slid her fingers into his. His palm was warm and dry as his grip closed around hers. She stepped towards the ledge, only vaguely aware of her surroundings. Everything else was centred on where their bodies connected. His free hand slipped around her waist and her breath caught in her throat. The next moment, she was lifted and gently set down next to him. As soon as she was steady, he dropped his arms; she was left feeling oddly bereft.

'It's not much further,' he murmured. He turned away from her and began walking again. She followed, her heart beating erratically as if she had just run a race. He walked on seemingly completely unperturbed by her touch. Of course, he would be. He was a Monceaux. Women must throw themselves at him, hoping to be in with a chance of joining one of the most influential families in the country, although that thought did him a disservice. He was a handsome man. Even without his family name, he must be used to women being all over him. He'd shown some interest in her but that was before he had told her the truth about himself.

Had the long looks and sparkling touches been a ploy to get to know her more? She shook her head. No, she didn't believe that. It was not possible to fake the attraction she had seen in his eyes. Desire wasn't their problem. Her body reacted to him whenever he was close and she did not doubt that he found her attractive in return. She could see it in his eyes. That did not mean she had to explore their mutual attraction. She wasn't so far in lust with him that her heart had to follow. She had only truly ever loved one person and that person was her son. The odd fluttering sensations in her stomach whenever she thought of or touched Al were not the same. It could not be romantic love. That was the stuff of legends, of courtly love and overblown poetry. When he left, she would be fine. She would not long for his company or think about the way he moved or his strength.

'We're here.'

'Where?' She looked about her. They were close to the beach now, but not among the rocks that touched the sand.

'Down here.'

He was pointing to a dark crevice. 'Another dark cave?'

She heard his laugh. 'I've made this one more comfortable than the last one we trekked through. I'll climb in first and then help you in.'

He crouched down; she couldn't see what happened next and then he'd disappeared. If she hadn't known he was there, she would have thought herself alone.

'Al.' She knelt, running her hands around the space, trying to find the opening.

'I'm right here.' The warmth of his fingers brushed the back of her hand. She laced her hands with his and he gently pulled her towards him.

'Careful of your head.'

She narrowly missed bumping her head on a jagged rock.

'There's no standing room. You'll need to lie beside me.'

She wriggled into the space, her feet going in first. When she'd pictured this evening, she'd imagined standing and then perhaps moving towards their quarry. She hadn't expected to be lying down. Al was right. The space was very tight. She tried to scoot away from him, but there was nowhere to go. The left side of her touched his from shoulder to toe. She didn't want to think about the way it made her feel, how his touch made her body feel alive. Not when he seemed completely unmoved by her presence.

'Here.' She felt him move and then a thick, fur-lined blanket settled over her shoulders.

'Thank you,' she murmured as her heart squeezed. He was so thoughtful. No one had ever taken care of her like this. Before Badon her parents had seen her as a way to make a treaty and had treated her much the same way they would an expensive rug. Badon had only seen her as a means for procreation. Now, everyone was so dependent on her being the leader that no one realised she needed to be taken care of every now and again. Everyone, that is, except Al.

'I came down earlier and made up a drilling exercise for some of the boys. I had a walk around and discovered I could hear them quite well from this vantage point.' Al's voice broke into her thoughts, reminding her that she had to concentrate. Her very life depended on it, which was why it was so frustrating that she kept thinking about Al.

'Good. Because we are not going to see very much in this darkness.'

'Yesterday, the men had a lantern. Hopefully, they will bring that with them. Do you know any of Yonescu's household enough to identify them?'

'I might. I don't go there very often. When we meet, he usually comes to me. I know his steward, but would he send someone so high up? But then, what am I saying? You have been sent on this mission and you are one of the leading men in the country.'

All down the length of her, she felt his body tense. 'I don't... I... It's not quite like that.'

'What do you mean?'

'I... It's nothing.'

'Are you hiding something else from me? Because if you are, I...' She paused. What could she threaten him with? Not much. 'I shall be very cross,' she finished halfheartedly.

'I wouldn't want that.' She heard the thread of amusement in his voice and she grimaced. She tried once again to move away from him but to no avail. 'I'm sorry,' he murmured. 'I didn't mean to upset you. I'm not hiding anything else from you.'

'Then what is it not quite like?'

She heard his long sigh. 'You never give up, do you?'

She frowned. 'I don't know what you mean.'

'You never let me get away with anything. You always question me. You could put the King's inquisitor out of a job. I'm not hiding anything that impacts you. There, will that do?'

She thought about it for a moment. 'No.'

He laughed quietly. 'It's going to have to.'

They settled into silence. Small waves washed onto the shore with a gentle hush. The men had to return tonight—they had to because she needed answers. She sighed. 'No. It's no good. I have to know.'

'I didn't even count a hundred.'

'You knew I was going to ask again?'

'Yes. I knew you weren't going to let it lie. This is personal. I'm not hiding something important from you. It's not something I've discussed with anyone else and it's not something I want to talk about now.'

He was weakening. She was sure of it. There had been no outright refusal this time. 'What does it matter if you tell me? Once you have found your man, you will be away and I will never see you again.' She ignored the black pit that opened in her heart at the thought. 'You might as well tell me.'

He grunted.

She went to ask again and then stopped. Being compared to the King's inquisitor was probably not a compliment. If it was personal, she would have to respect that and not question him any further. She bit her lips together to stop herself from asking again.

'I'm not good enough.'

She turned to him. 'What?'

'I shouldn't be in the King's Knights. I'm not good enough.'

She twisted towards him. 'Don't be ridiculous. The King's Knights are the most elite fighting group in the country. Their exploits are legendary. The travelling bards tell tales about the group of knights who protect the King. You could not be one of them if you were not good enough.'

She felt him shrug. 'My brother is Sir Benedictus. He is the leader of the knights. That is why I am in the group. I've told you before, I have no special talents.'

She snorted. 'You have many talents.'

'Not in comparison to the other knights.' His voice was calm and reasonable but she thought she could detect an undertone, a fathomless sadness she had not heard from him before.

'I don't believe you. I have never seen anyone with your strength. You must be worth at least five men when it comes to a fight.'

'There are men as big as me. The rest of the knights are skilled warriors. My size does not make me special.'

'That is not true. I have never seen—'

'You have never been to Windsor. You have never seen an elite fighting force. Trust me, I am nothing special in that regard.'

Johanne frowned. How could a man she'd come to think of as nearly faultless have such a twisted opinion of himself? 'It's true I have never been to Windsor, but I have seen fighters. You are exceptional.'

'Exceptionally big doesn't mean exceptionally clever. Benedictus is a master of strategy. Theo can spot a lie from across the room and there is no better protector than Will. All of them are gifted fighters. I am not looking for sympathy or for you to think you must make me feel better. I have long since accepted it.'

How infuriating. 'Mmm…'

'What does that mean?'

'It means nothing.'

He nudged her with his shoulder. 'Never has a sound had such loaded meaning.'

She huffed. 'It means, I think you are talking absolute rot.'

He stiffened. 'I see, and your vast knowledge…'

'I do not have to have travelled to know what I know.'

'And what is it that you know?' His voice had an edge to it now but she wasn't scared of him. He was the exact opposite of Badon. He would not hurt her even though he was irritated. He would never use his strength to bend innocent people to his will. He did not realise what a truly exceptional man he was.

'I know lots of things.' And now she sounded like Cineas trying to win an argument. 'I know that you put others before yourself.'

He snorted. 'That is hardly a special talent. Chivalry is an oath all knights must make at their dubbing. Honour, loyalty and politeness to all is part of the knightly code of conduct.'

'You go further than that.'

'I—'

'No, don't argue with me.' She had to make him see. 'It's true. Your size and strength could

frighten children and yet I have seen the way
you are with the young ones. You bend down
to talk to them, especially Cineas; you lower
your voice and change your body language.
Not many would make such an effort.'

He shifted next to her, as if her words made
him uncomfortable, but she wasn't finished. If
the only thing to come out of this strange ex-
pedition was that he saw himself the way she
did, then the night would be a success.

'Then there is the way you have helped me
with Brae. Making sure that Brae is safe from
Morcant.'

'Again, the code of chivalry—'

She growled in frustration. 'Not all knights
follow the code.'

For a moment, he said nothing. She listened
to his breathing as he pondered what she'd
said. 'Well, they should,' he said eventually.

She groaned. 'You are so frustrating. Why
can't you see that you are different?'

'I may be different but I am not exceptional.
Not like—'

'If I asked your brother knights, what would
they say about you?'

'How would I know?' he asked gruffly. 'It

is not like we sit around and talk about each other. There is always much work to be done.'

'We have lots of time to spare. Humour me and answer the question.'

He huffed out a breath. 'Fine. Theo would say that I am always calm before a battle, that my presence with the troops prevents panic from setting in. Will would say that my bulk frightens witnesses into talking as soon as they set eyes on me, making his job easier. Benedictus would praise my strength but there would be a look in his eye, which would make me question whether that was enough for him.'

She nodded slowly. 'So, it is Benedictus who is the reason you doubt yourself because the other two are very complimentary.'

'Yes. In this completely imaginary scenario, I suppose they are.'

Johanne ignored that. 'Has your brother actually come out and said anything to support your belief that he doesn't think you are good enough?'

'He doesn't need to. He has the exact same look our father had whenever I disappointed him, which was often before you ask. He wanted another mastermind for his second son, an exact replica of Benedictus. What he got was a brute.'

'You are not a brute. You are a kind and honest man with a formidable body.' She hadn't meant to add that last part. Her comment about his body had come out like a soft caress. Heat spread across her cheeks and she was glad for the dark so that he could not see the expression on her face. She had to hope he had missed the longing in her voice.

She heard him swallow. 'Johanne.'

'Your belief that you are not good enough isn't justified,' she said briskly, brushing away her moment of tenderness. 'You may not have noticed but you were the one who thought to destroy the trebuchet, you are the man who has transformed Brae into a castle which could withstand a siege. A strong wind would have blown it down before.'

'Mmm.'

Unsure whether that was a good noise or not, she carried on. 'It's also you who reasoned that Yonescu is behind the treasonous plot. I would have persisted in seeing Morcant as the traitor. You found this cave…'

He laughed. 'All right, I see your point. Does this mean…' He cleared his throat. 'You have been very generous to me just now. May I hope that this means I am forgiven for not telling you the truth about my reason for being at Brae?'

She sighed softly. 'I understand why you did what you did. It was your mission and you cannot break your oath to our King.'

'Thank you.'

'I didn't say you were forgiven.'

He laughed lightly and she nudged his shoulder. 'I suppose I can forgive you. You have done much good work around Brae. It would be churlish to hold a grudge when you have done so much for me and my people.'

There was a pause. 'Johanne, you are... I want...' His voice was laden with an emotion she did not understand but which caused a strange, squirming sensation to start up in her stomach.

She waited but he said nothing more and they lapsed into silence.

An age passed. Her legs became stiff but she didn't dare move. She wanted him to say something, anything to break the silence between them. But he didn't. Gradually, her eyelids became heavy. She tried to keep them open, tried to focus on the moment, but her eyes closed, once, twice and then they didn't open again.

She woke abruptly when Al grabbed her arm.

'What is it?' she said, her voice laced with sleep.

'Down there. I think I can see a light.' Something flickered at the far end of the beach. 'It's getting closer.'

Johanne held her breath as the flicker resolved itself into a torch. 'It's them. It has to be.'

'We'll need to be quiet,' he whispered.

'Of course. Sorry.' Sleep had robbed her of her senses and she spoke out loud again.

She felt his grumble ripple through him. She went to apologise but managed to close her mouth before the words came out. Voices reached them but they were too faint to make out any fine details. They appeared to stop moving. She wriggled her toes. If only they could get closer.

Johanne shifted and Alewyn stifled a groan. The small cave was a disaster. When he'd found it earlier, he'd congratulated himself on finding somewhere so secluded yet offering such a fantastic view. He had given no thought to the size of the space. Hadn't for one moment considered what it would do to him, to lie so close to Johanne and not be able to touch her. Despite their thick clothes and despite the rug, he was conscious only of her curves. Not the cold, not the discomfort and not even the importance of the mission could break through his desire to turn to her and take her in his arms, to blot out everything with a taste of her lips.

It had almost been a relief to talk about his failings. To discuss all the reasons why he was not good enough for the King's Knights. But she had argued with him there, picking apart his reasoning and pointing out why he was wrong. Part of him was irritated. He had held these views about himself for so long they had almost become part of him. But as she'd spoken, he'd listened and his heart had lightened. Perhaps she was right. Perhaps he did have qualities which raised him above a normal knight, which made him worthy of his place amongst the King's Knights. And when she had said she had forgiven him, he had wanted nothing more than to take her in his arms and forget everything—his mission, his family and the threat of Morcant. None of it mattered in comparison. Fortunately, his common sense had prevailed and he had managed to stop himself from making an utter fool of himself. She may want him for a momentary distraction but she had made it absolutely clear she did not want a man in her life. Alewyn had a horrible feeling that if he let her get any closer to him, he would not be able to stop himself from falling in love.

He would think on what she had said about him later, when he was alone and not driven to distraction by her closeness. For now, he needed all his years of training to concentrate on what was happening below. The people on the beach still weren't getting any closer and Johanne's fidgeting was getting worse.

He leaned close to her ear, inadvertently inhaling her scent; his body tightened with desire and he closed his eyes. He needed to get away from her. If he had a break from her presence, even for a day, it would hopefully stop this overwhelming need for her that swamped him whenever he got close. He swallowed, forcing himself to ignore what his body wanted. 'Don't fret. They will have to come closer.'

She turned to him, her face so close her breath brushed across his lips. 'Why?'

He should move away. Should put himself out of the reach of temptation. Instead, he leaned closer, his lips almost touching hers. 'From up on the cliff, it's easier to see than from this angle, but close to us is the only part of the bay accessible by boat. The rest is too rocky. If these are our men, they will come to us.'

He should move away, should stop her mouth from connecting with his. But he didn't. He was tired of fighting his desire, tired of telling himself he couldn't touch her. In this moment, there was no reason on earth why he couldn't. Her lips brushed his and he was lost. Her kiss was soft and tentative but it burned against his skin, consuming him and urging him to take more.

His hand slipped into her hair at the base of her neck, and the silky tendrils fell off his fingers. He used his thumb to trace the delicate skin of her jaw and tilted his head for better access to her mouth.

Her lips parted and he swept his tongue inside, tasting her. The soft moan she made was his undoing. All sense of the world outside fell away; there was only her lips and the press of her body against his.

A shout from the beach had them pulling apart. For a moment, he couldn't remember where he was and what on earth he was meant to be doing. A splash in the water beyond had him turning his gaze to the beach. 'Damn it.'

The men had moved to just below him and he hadn't noticed, his craving for this woman making him lose his mind at the most crucial moment. Thankfully, they hadn't missed whatever was happening this evening but he could easily have done so. A boat was a short distance from the shore. The men on the beach were watching its approach, not talking and unmoving.

If the oarsman had not made the splash, he would have missed it because he was following his body's infatuation and not his mission. *That* was why he had to stay away from Johanne. She may be beautiful and intriguing but distraction by her meant he lost his focus. It was all well and good her telling him that he was worthy of his place in the King's Knights but he had to prove it to himself.

'This has to be it?' Johanne's voice was full of excitement.

'Yes.'

From the flickering light the men carried with them, Alewyn could just about make out the two men from the beach wading into the water and grabbing hold of the boat before pulling it up out of the water and onto the sand. If Alewyn hadn't been watching and listening intently, he wouldn't have known anything was afoot. This tiny little cove in Brae really was the perfect place to bring Frenchmen discreetly into the country.

Alewyn's heart began to pound as two men clambered out of the boat. There was the deep rumble of voices and then the boat was pushed back into the water. The exchange had lasted barely any time at all.

The men on the beach moved closer towards their hiding place. At last, Alewyn was able to hear snatches of conversation.

'...head north...'

'...clothes and food in a bag...'

'...a contact will meet you outside...'

Johanne inhaled sharply.

He leaned over and spoke into her ear. 'What is it?'

'The man who just spoke, he is Yonescu's steward. I thought he had died last year. Yonescu has been bringing someone else with him ever since,' she whispered.

'Are you sure?'

She paused for a moment. 'Yes. I am sure.' She gripped his arm. 'Is this the proof we need?'

'It's a start.' For the first time since he had woken confused and missing significant parts of his memory, he felt the first stirrings of hope. This could be the beginning of the end of the mission. The moment he proved to himself and his family that he was worthy of his place in the King's Knights.

The men were moving down the beach now, away from him. 'I'm going to follow them. First, I will need to borrow a horse, if you will permit it, of course.'

'You may, but I will come too.'

'No.' She flinched from the harshness of his words but he couldn't afford to feel guilty. He couldn't have her with him any more. Her presence was clouding his judgement. When she was around all he could think of was her, craving her touch or her laugh, or even just her attention. It was no good. 'Your people need you here. You need to keep preparing for the siege.' He began to scramble out of the cave. Her grip slipped off his arm; he wished he didn't feel the loss of her touch so acutely but he assured himself that need would fade. All he needed was distance. He stood and stretched, relieving his aching limbs. Further down the beach, the flicker of light was reaching the edge of the beach. He had to hurry. Johanne crawled out after him and pushed herself to her feet.

'Will you come back?'

'I will.' He would, even if this trip resolved his mission. He would make sure Brae was fully secure before he returned to Windsor. That was the right thing to do and had nothing to do with the yawning pit that opened up inside him at the thought of not seeing her one more time before he returned to his normal life.

'You will be safe.'

'Of course, this is the bit I *am* good at.'

She didn't respond. As they hurried back to the castle to fetch a horse, he wished he could read her mind. Was she asking about his return because she wanted to see him? She had kissed him after all, but she had made it very clear, time and again, she did not want a man in her life. Not that he was offering. No matter how much she appealed to him, she was not part of his future. He was so near to proving to his brother that he did belong in the King's Knights. This was what he'd been aiming for, for so long.

Chapter Twelve

Johanne rolled over on her mattress and flopped onto her back. Sleep wouldn't come, no matter how much her bones ached. Two days had passed since she'd said goodbye to Al. Two days of stocking up on food and water, of checking over weapons' stores and making sure the men she and Al had picked were ready to face the siege that was coming. Two days of worrying about what was taking him so long. Yonescu's land was not so far away from hers that it should have taken two whole days for him to get there and back.

She pushed herself to a sitting position. It was no good. She could not sleep and she could not blame it on the worry of Morcant and his ridiculous plans to take over her castle.

No, it was not that which stopped her from

sleeping. Whenever she closed her eyes, she pictured Al, lying motionless on the road like she'd found him, only this time he wasn't breathing. The fear that flooded through her caused her stomach to churn. Deep down, she knew he was strong, far stronger than anyone she had ever met, and she knew he was good at sneaking about despite his size, but he was only one man. If he'd been caught by Yonescu and his associates, then she may never discover what happened to him.

She wished she'd had the courage to invite him to her bed. She didn't want a husband but that shouldn't mean she should deny herself the opportunity for some company. She had a feeling Al would be able to show her exactly what the women of her castle giggled about when they discussed relations with a man. She at least wished she had tried to find out.

She climbed down from the bed and slipped into her boots. The fire in her chamber had died down and cold air nipped at her skin. Searching around she found her cloak. Pulling it over her nightclothes, she made her way towards the door. If she was up, she may as well do a surprise check on her new guards to make sure none of them were sleeping on the job. So far, her people had surpassed her expectations but the calm they were living in was a false environment and, at present, there was a jovial camaraderie as they all worked against an unseen enemy. The real pressure would show when Morcant arrived. Then they would see who would manage to stay awake and who would not.

Her boots clipped on the stone staircase as she made her way down. She stopped outside Al's room. The door was slightly ajar. Without giving herself time to think, she pushed it open and stepped inside.

There was no fire in the grate. The blankets Al had slept in were arranged neatly on the mattress; the floor was clean. It was as if he had never been there. She crouched down next to his bed and lifted the top blanket. Muttering words which cursed her own foolishness, she bent her head and inhaled. The fabric still had the faint hint of his scent and longing pooled in her stomach.

'What are you doing?'

'Ahh!' she screamed, whirling round to face the intruder.

A large shape blocked the doorway.

'Al.' Without thinking she raced towards him.

He lifted her as she threw her arms around him. His lips came down on hers and her body exploded with sensation. They had kissed before but there had always been some reason for them to stop. Not this time. She wanted to know him, know everything about him before he left her for ever. This was a pleasure she wanted to take for herself before the horror of the future took over.

She ran her hands over his shoulders and down the length of his arms. Soft moans filled the room and she realised they were coming from her. She'd never realised there could be such pleasure from the touching of mouths and, now she knew, she wanted more of it. She tugged at his cloak, wanting it off, wanting less material between them. She wanted to run her hands over his body, to know if his muscled arms felt as good as she had spent so much time imagining them to be.

Gripping her with one arm, he managed to divest himself of his cloak. It landed on the floor with a thud but she barely noticed. Even his tunic was too much clothing.

She hadn't registered they were moving. Not until they tumbled onto the mattress. He twisted so that she fell on top of him, cushioning her fall. She didn't want to break the kiss but she needed to touch his skin more than she needed to breathe.

She pushed herself upright and gazed down at him. His eyes were nearly completely black, his lips swollen. He grinned up at her and laughter gurgled out of her. He leaned up and claimed her mouth anew. She began to pull at his clothes, tearing them from his body. He moaned as her fingers splayed across the width of his chest.

'Slow down,' he murmured. She ignored him. She wanted to touch him everywhere, to memorise the shape of him.

He laughed and captured her wrists in one of his large hands. 'I haven't ached for you for so long only to rush. I want to savour this.'

His lips were tilted in that half-smile of his. The one that made her heart flutter strangely. He lightly touched his lips to hers and then lowered her down onto the mattress, reversing their positions.

'You are so beautiful.' His tone was full of

wonder and her heart swelled. No one had ever spoken to her with such reverence before.

'I'm going to let go of your hands but you must promise me to keep them still.'

'But I...'

Laughter glinted in his eyes. 'No arguing with me, Johanne. If you keep up with that wild touching, this will be over before I get a chance to appreciate you in the way you deserve.'

She swallowed. 'I promise to keep my hands to myself.'

'Good.'

'For now.'

His laugh brushed over her skin as he leaned down and lightly kissed the base of her neck. 'I guess that will have to do.'

Slowly, he let go of her hands. She kept her word and left them above her head. He sat back on his heels and looked down at her. Somewhere along the way, she had lost the cloak she'd been wearing and was now only in her undergarments. The fabric pulled tight across her body, showing her curves. His gaze flickered over her body and a muscle tightened in his jaw. He briefly closed his eyes and then let out a long breath. 'You are so lovely.'

He opened his eyes and they locked with hers. Her breath caught in her throat from the intensity of his look. Keeping his gaze on her face, he moved his hands down to her ankles. She moaned as his hands finally touched her skin, the sound deep and throaty.

Alewyn's fingers trembled as he slipped them over Johanne's skin. Her calves were tiny in his hands, her skin soft and warm. Her eyelids fluttered shut as he ran his hands up, over her thighs, her hips, her tiny waist, pushing the fabric of her clothes up. She was breathing quickly now, as if she had run a race.

Her nipples puckered as he exposed her breasts to the cold night air. He bent his head and took one into his mouth. She bucked off the bed, crying out. His body edged even closer to release and he knew he needed to slow things down. They would not have long together. He needed to return to Windsor as a matter of urgency, but he knew that he wanted this, knew that he couldn't walk away from her now. His self-restraint had disappeared the moment she had thrown herself into his arms. A small part of him tried to remind himself why he shouldn't do this, why his heart might be in danger, but his body overrode his objections. He craved her touch, needed it more than anything.

He rocked back up and she moaned, 'Don't stop.'

'Only for a moment.' He pulled her clothes the rest of the way off her and gazed down at her. He'd imagined her a thousand different times, but the reality was even better.

Unable to help himself, he began to touch her again. Tracing his fingers over the sensitive flesh of her stomach, the underside of her breast, her beautifully taut nipples. For every pass of his hand, her grip on the covers tightened.

'Please. I...'

'What is it that you want, Johanne?' He loved this. Loved that he could make her insensible with barely a touch.

'I want more...'

'Here?' Running his fingers over the curve of her breast.

'Yes...and...' She arched into his touch.

'Is there somewhere else?'

'Yes... I...' She moaned as his hand travelled down, over the curve of her stomach to the coppery curls at the junction of her thighs.

He wanted to taste her there but he was at the very edge of his control now. He wanted to be inside her more than he wanted to live.

'Here?' he asked, his hand between her legs, skimming over the softness.

She cried out. 'Oh. Al, is that... I never knew...'

His soul crowed in triumph, knowing that he was the first to make her feel like this.

Her eyes flew open, her gaze connecting with his. 'I want you inside me.'

'Always so bossy.' He bent down and claimed her mouth. Her hands slipped into his hair, holding him in place. For long, delicious moments their tongues tangled as his hand moved over her.

'Johanne,' he murmured against her mouth.

'Mmm.' She ran her lips down the column of his throat.

'I'm very big and you're so tiny. I do not want to crush you.'

Her tongue ran over his nipple and he very nearly lost control there and then.

'I don't care.' She tried to pull him down but he held firm.

'I'd like to try something. I think this will be better for you.'

Her hands were beginning to explore him again, her promise to keep them still forgotten. 'Very well. Whatever you like,' she whispered against his chest and his heart tightened. She was so trusting of him; perhaps there was hope for them after all. Maybe she would consider… Her hand brushed the length of him and he lost all thoughts apart from the desire to be one with her.

He moved away from her, smiling at her grunt of displeasure. Very gently, he rolled her onto her front. Kneeling behind her, he lifted her hips slightly off the bed. She moaned and that was his undoing. With one hand on the mattress, propping himself upright, and the other at her hip, he slowly eased into her.

'Are you…?' he breathed when he was fully in.

'Yes,' she breathed. 'More…'

He began to move then, his hand continuing to stroke her as his body took over. Everything else disappeared until there was only her and her cries of delight, and when she toppled over the edge, he followed her, his world becoming nothing but exquisite pleasure.

Johanne was warm, warmer than she had been in days. Her body was contented and, for once, she had woken without fear pressing down on her. Her muscles ached deliciously. She rolled over and hit something solid. Her eyes sprung open. She was pressed against Al's shoulder. His naked shoulder. Images from earlier came back to her. Al, his hands touching her, awakening sensations she'd never experienced and hadn't known were possible. The ache that had built between her legs and the way he had satisfied that with care and a passion that had taken her breath away. Now she knew, now she understood, and she was glad for it.

Al was breathing evenly but somehow she knew he was not asleep. She looked up. He was gazing down at her, an unreadable expression in his eyes. She licked her lips and something flickered in the depths of his eyes.

He cleared his throat. 'Johanne.'

She smiled, her heart squeezing. 'Alewyn.'

He smiled softly. 'I should tell you about what I found out today, or perhaps it was yesterday. I have lost track of time.'

'Oh, yes.' She didn't want him to tell her anything that wasn't related to them right here and now. She didn't want the real world to intrude on this moment but she couldn't tell him that, couldn't let him know how it felt to be here with him. She didn't want him to know that he had come to mean more to her than she had ever thought possible. She trusted him, knew that he would take care of her if she let him, but part of her held back from giving him too much. Even though he was not Badon, he was still a man. If she gave him her heart, no matter how good a man he was, he would still want control. That was the way of the world. And the little niggle that suggested Al would be different had to be ignored. She couldn't take that chance.

'Yonescu's steward headed straight for Yonescu's stronghold while the two Frenchmen headed north. I followed the steward and his friend and I got lucky. Yonescu met them outside his castle, after making them wait a day.'

'Why would he do that?'

Al shrugged. 'Perhaps he got caught up in something else or they arrived early. Maybe he just enjoys the power. Not all his household can be involved in the plot and so believe, like you, that the man is dead. Whatever the reason, Yonescu obviously doesn't want everyone to know he is conducting treasonous acts. There will be some amongst his household who are loyal to the King. The two men left after they spoke with him and headed southwest.'

'Yonescu is definitely in on it then?'

Al nodded. 'Yes, I am afraid so. I didn't overhear everything—I had to keep my distance—but I heard enough to know that Yonescu has full knowledge of the operation. I am not sure, but from what I overheard, I believe his motivation is financial rather than political.'

A strange pang touched her heart. She'd thought Yonescu was, if not her friend, then at least her supporter. She should have known better. She was on her own. She always had been and that is how she would always be.

'What happens now?' Her heart hurt, dreading the answer but knowing what was inevitable.

'Now I must return to Windsor and report my findings to Benedictus.' There was no sadness in his voice. It did not sound as if he was loath to leave her and Brae.

Johanne pushed the pain of him going to one side. She had always known this would happen and so she had no right to be sad. He had done more for her than anyone else had ever done and she was grateful.

'What will happen to Yonescu?'

'He will hang.'

Johanne shivered and Al pulled her closer. She curled into the warmth of his body.

'The man has manipulated you, Johanne. There is no need to worry about his immortal soul. He was not worried about you when he pitted you and Morcant against one another in order to distract you. He was thinking only of himself.'

'I know. I understand.'

He ran a hand up her back. She had never thought of herself as a small woman—she was taller than most—but he made her feel tiny, and the way he worshipped her body made her feel special and cherished.

'Johanne...'

'Mmm?' She traced his chest with her lips. Goose bumps broke out across his skin and she smiled.

'We should talk about this.' His voice sounded breathy and not at all like what she was used to.

'What is there to say?' she murmured. She ran her tongue around his nipple and he inhaled sharply.

'We should...' He groaned as her fingers lightly skimmed over his erection and she grinned in satisfaction. He had reduced her to a boneless state. It was time to do the same thing to him, if she could. She had never managed such a feat before but it couldn't be difficult. All she had to do was listen to how his body responded to hers. From the sound of his breathing, she was doing just fine.

'What we are doing…it normally takes place in…' His breathing was fast now. Her hand closed around him. 'It normally takes place in a marriage bed,' he ground out.

She froze. 'Marriage,' she whispered against his chest.

'Yes. No, please don't put up those barriers again.' He brushed a strand of hair away from her face. He was holding himself very still now; she could see the effort it was costing him in the taut muscles of his neck.

'What barriers?'

She stroked him and his eyes rolled to the back of his head. A thrill of triumph ripped through her and she bent to touch her mouth to his. His hand came up to cup her head as their kiss quickly became heated. He pulled himself away, his breathing heavy. 'Stop distracting me. I'm talking about the wall you keep around you to keep yourself from getting hurt.'

'I don't—'

'You do. And there's no need.' His lips brushed hers. 'Your people love and respect you. They do not need you to be tough all the time. They like you as you are. *I* like you as you are. I know that you don't want to get married again but there could be a babe and…'

Her heart stuttered. He was good and kind; how like him to offer to marry her. Many men wouldn't after they had taken their pleasure. 'You mustn't worry about a babe. My bleeding stopped last night. I will not conceive. And about the walls I put around myself…you are right. I will try and stop doing that but for now let us…' Her hand moved over his length and she revelled in the way he shuddered.

'But…'

No. She did not want to talk about this. Al was a good man, but he was still a man and from a powerful family. Brae would become swallowed up by him and she would have no control over her future. 'Let us just enjoy tonight.'

'But…'

She nudged him with her hand and he obliged her by rolling fully onto his back. She was glad, for she knew that she was incapable of moving him herself.

She straddled his body. 'Now it is my turn to touch you.'

His lips tilted, although there was a look in his eyes she could not decipher. 'As you wish, my lady.'

'It is also your turn to keep your hands by your sides.'

He frowned. 'I am not sure I can promise that.'

She leaned down and lightly brushed her lips over his. 'You must.'

'I'll keep my promise for as long as you kept yours.'

She laughed. 'I had better get started then.'

Chapter Thirteen

'You have done well. Everything is looking prepared.' Al smiled down at Johanne as he spoke. She tried to smile back even as his words sounded so final.

Al had stayed at Brae for one more day and they had had one more night together, but she had seen that faraway look in his eyes and known that now he needed to leave. He hadn't mentioned marriage to her again. Part of her wanted to question him, to ask if he'd really meant to ask her or whether the offer had been made when he'd been at his most content, when a union between the two of them had seemed like a good idea. Or perhaps he had felt obliged to offer her marriage after they had lain together and had felt nothing but relief when she had insisted they enjoy their time together and not marry. Mostly, she was relieved he hadn't mentioned it again. She had resolved to stay unwed but, deep down, she knew that if Al had pressed the issue she may not have been able to resist.

Marriage to Al would be different. They knew how to please each other, which would be a marked improvement on her first marriage, but it was more than just physical satisfaction. Al would be kind to her and her people, she was sure of that. He would not dominate her or those who depended on Brae but Brae would never come first for him. His priority would always be the King and the knights who served him. And that was fine, that was what Al had sworn an oath to do. She did not hold it against him or want to change him in any way. But she would not be second best. She would rather be alone, controlling her own destiny, than be someone's afterthought. She owed herself that much.

Now he was going, and she hadn't expected his parting to hurt so much. There were no more reasons for him to stay and a very pressing reason to go. Treason against the King was far more important than her small territory.

That was her own private tragedy—nothing in the grand scheme of things.

'Thank you for everything you've done.' Her thanks were inadequate. He had done so much: protected her when she'd needed it, helped to shore up Brae's defences and proved she was not guilty of treason, which prevented her from the hangman's noose. And he had given her her first real taste of pleasure.

He continued to smile down at her, his eyes filling with warmth. 'Thank you for pulling me off the path and for taking me in. Without you, I am sure I would have died. Here, I want you to have this.' He handed her the silver buckle that normally clasped his cloak together. The metal was warm from his touch. 'It's worth something. You could melt it down or sell it as it is. It's only a small token of my appreciation for taking me in when you could have left me to die on that very first day.'

She clutched the clasp tightly. She knew she would never sell it or melt it down. This was something she would keep with her, to remember him in the years to come. 'I have barely done anything for you.' Her words sounded far harsher than she intended; she didn't miss his wince. 'I mean that you have done more for me. The castle, it looks better than I have ever seen it. Some of my men will do well in the coming siege. We stand a chance, something we didn't without your help.'

He smiled, although this time it didn't reach his eyes. 'I must be going.'

She nodded, unable to speak past the lump in her throat, not wanting to betray how much his leaving was cleaving her heart in two.

It was right that he go. He did not belong to her. She did not belong to him. They were not meant to be together for any longer. She would not see him again.

'Johanne...'

She looked up and caught his gaze. He was frowning. 'Johanne, I really wish you—'

'Lady Johanne, Sir Alewyn...' A voice called them from the other side of the courtyard. They both turned.

Gemel was walking towards them, a sack in his hands. 'I wanted to ask you before you left...' Gemel carried on talking but Johanne didn't hear anything. Her last moment with Al was over and whatever he had been about to say to her was lost.

Gemel didn't leave as Al swung onto the horse he had borrowed from Brae, and Gemel didn't leave her side as the three of them made their way to Brae's exit.

Most of the castle inhabitants had gathered to see him off. They did not know where he was going, only that it was vital for him to leave. Johanne had not wanted her people to hate him for going when they might need him most. When the threat of Morcant was over, she would tell her people the truth. For now, she had decided to be tight-lipped. They did not need to know that he would not be back.

Al thanked everyone for their hard work over the last ten days. He praised the men he'd trained and told them they would prevail.

He did not promise to return.

And then he was gone in a clatter of hooves.

She watched as he rode down and away from Brae and she watched as he disappeared into the forest that would eventually take him to the road to London. She watched as her heart splintered. He didn't turn around once.

Chapter Fourteen

The bright skies of the south turned grey and dull as Alewyn approached Windsor. The smell coming from the large settlement clogged his throat and made him long for the salty, fresh air of the coast.

The horse he had borrowed was close to giving up, but they had less than a league to go and then they could both rest. He urged the mount on; it trudged over the ground, its demeanour matching the state of Alewyn's heart.

A rider was coming towards him, his stiff posture giving away his brother's identity long before Alewyn could get a clear look at the man's face.

Benedictus's frown was so deep small children could get lost in it. There was not a hint of warmth in his brother's eyes as they finally came into speaking distance. 'I thought you were dead,' Benedictus growled.

Unsure of what to say to that, Alewyn remained silent.

'A week ago, your horse arrived with all your belongings. She looked like she had been in a battle.'

'I see you rushed out to discover the truth.' It shouldn't hurt that his safety wasn't his brother's immediate concern, but it did.

Benedictus's lips twisted. 'Unfortunately, I am not in a position to abandon everything for personal matters. I had to wait for Theo to return before I could leave.'

For the first time, Alewyn noticed that his brother was indeed dressed for travel. Muscles in his back that he hadn't realised were tense slowly relaxed. His brother was the most senior knight in the country. He could not leave his post, that much was true. Yet here he was. On the road to Brae to look for him.

'Let us return to the castle. I have much to tell you.'

'Did you find enough evidence to hang Lady Johanne?'

Alewyn's fingers tightened on his reins. 'I did not.' Was it his imagination, or did his brother's body sag with disappointment at his statement? If so, was that disappointment in Alewyn or in the lack of evidence to hang Johanne? Did Benedictus think he'd failed in his mission? Alewyn waited for the familiar feelings of inadequacy to hit. He was so used to feeling that way whenever presented with Benedictus's disappointment. They didn't come. Whether that was because he knew this time that he could prove to his brother that the mission had been a success or whether it was because of something else, Alewyn didn't know. He only knew that it was a relief. Whatever shadow he had been living under for so long had gone.

'Very well. We will return to the castle. You can tell me everything in the presence of Theo.'

Alewyn didn't question that, Theo was their master questioner. He could get you to answer questions you did not even know you knew the answer to.

'In what way was Ffleur hurt?'

'There were cuts to her legs.' Alewyn nodded. That was consistent with the rope Johanne had found. Alewyn's heart twisted at the thought of Ffleur suffering without him there to help her. 'There was no damage to her bulk, although her coat had become matted. It was nothing the stable master was not able to fix. As far as I can tell, your belongings were all there.'

'And my sword?'

'It was strapped to Ffleur.' There was a pause. 'That was what convinced me you must be dead. You never travel without it.'

For the first time, Alewyn heard some emotion in his brother's voice. Perhaps the old devil did have a heart after all.

If Ffleur and he had not ridden into the trap, Johanne and Gemel would have fallen foul of it. Whatever the plan had been, to frighten them or worse, then Alewyn could only be glad it was he who had come across it first. He would rather be hurt a thousand times over than any harm befall her.

He and Benedictus did not speak for the rest of their journey. It reminded Alewyn of his childhood before he had left to do his knight's training. Back then, it had been his parents who'd used silence as a weapon. People often thought shouting was the most effective punishment for a young child but his parents had used their quietness like a knife. Benedictus had been his comrade-in-arms in those days, had looked out for him when their parents had turned on him. Now, Alewyn doubted Benedictus was trying to punish him, but he could still hear his disapproval in the lack of any comment. Strangely, the silence didn't bother Alewyn. Perhaps that was also because he knew he had all the answers this time. His mission had been a success and now all he had to do was impart his knowledge and he would prevent a war on English soil.

Or perhaps there was another reason for his new-found calm. He had tried hard not to think of Johanne as he had ridden towards Windsor. The two nights he had spent in her arms had been the best of his life but it was not only her body that he missed. Several times on the long ride, he had turned to her to ask her opinion or to pass the time of day and she had not been there. The loss had left him feeling winded. Johanne had not just been his friend; she had given him something precious. She had given him a belief in himself and his abilities and he would be grateful to her for ever for that.

He had mentioned marriage and she had brushed him off. It had hurt him more than he would have thought possible but the pain had been dulled by the pleasure of her body. He'd thought about mentioning it again, had tried to just before he had left Brae, but he'd been thwarted by the arrival of her steward. He could have pressed the issue but he hadn't. She had seemed content to leave their relationship at what had passed between them and he hadn't wanted to sully their last moments together with an argument or, worse, a kind rejection. Because he knew she would not agree to marry him no matter how much he might want to be joined with her for the rest of his life. He told himself to be glad. He did not want or need the commitment of marriage right now.

As the leagues had lengthened between her and Windsor, he pondered on what had passed between them and thought he might have made a mistake. He had mentioned marriage but he had not asked her. Perhaps he should have done. No, perhaps he should have *begged* her to come with him. But deep down he knew she did not want to be anywhere other than Brae. Besides, she refused to be beholden to a man and he respected that. He would never have treated her like her late husband, never try to bend her to his will, but there had been no point reiterating that. His place was here, hers was there. He would have to learn to live without her.

Theo's double take when he saw him made Alewyn laugh out loud. His brother knight pulled him into a fierce hug. 'We thought you were dead.' Theo slapped him on the back and released him. 'I am glad you are not.'

Alewyn grinned. 'Me too.'

'Don't scare us like that again or I'll be forced to hunt you down and kill you myself.'

Alewyn laughed as he followed the men deeper into Windsor Castle, towards Benedictus's private chamber where he conducted all his business. This room was small and functional with the most uncomfortable benches known to man for everyone, apart from Benedictus, to sit on. Instead of subjecting himself to that torture, Alewyn made his way over to the fire and began to warm his body in the powerful heat.

Benedictus settled in his chair behind his desk. 'Tell me everything.'

Alewyn stared at the flickering flames. He'd had plenty of time to get the story straight in his mind. He wanted it to be completely clear that there was no doubt that Johanne was innocent of any plot against the King. Yet, he didn't want to reveal all he had done to help her prepare for the siege. He would downplay that part.

He turned and almost took a seat on the bench. He was tired after riding for nearly three days straight, only stopping to rest when his horse could go no further. Before he could lower himself, he remembered how the bench seemed to take delight in torturing him and he remained standing. Leaning against the wall, he gave a succinct retelling of everything that had happened to him from the moment he had left Windsor until his return, explaining that some of the events before Lady Johanne had picked him up were still patchy.

'What do you think happened to make you unconscious on the path?' asked Theo when he stopped.

'I'll never know for sure. My best guess is that Ffleur ran into a rope that was set to unseat someone else and threw me off. I was black and blue when I regained consciousness, although nothing was broken.'

'A de-seating wouldn't normally do you much damage.' Benedictus's gaze flicked over his body. 'But there was that storm not long after you left, so perhaps you are right. It is unlikely that anyone would attack you, then leave you alive and not take any of your belongings.' Benedictus leaned forward, Alewyn's accident already dismissed from his mind. 'Arresting Yonescu is a priority but first we must find these Frenchmen before they can do any harm. Do you know where they were headed?'

'Towards Cranleigh.' Alewyn named a settlement he knew to be south of Windsor.

'We will assemble some men and hunt them down. Then we will focus on Yonescu and he will know the full displeasure of the King's Knights. As for Lady Johanne, we will leave her in peace.'

Alewyn braced himself against the wall, glad to have the support as his knees turned to liquid. He'd thought his brother would believe him about Johanne but to have the confirmation that no one would go after her or anyone at Brae brought him bone-weakening relief.

Theo was watching him, a slight smirk on his lips. 'Lady Johanne got mentioned rather a lot during that recitation.'

Alewyn glared at Theo. 'I was staying at her castle and she was one of the main suspects in the treasonous plot. Of course her name was mentioned a lot.'

Theo's smirk became a grin. 'Was she pretty by any chance?'

Alewyn's heart began to race. Was Theo about to bring down all the good Alewyn had done by implying Alewyn was attracted to Johanne? If Benedictus realised just how lovely Alewyn thought Johanne was, it could negate everything he'd done thus far. 'Whether she is beautiful or not is neither here nor there.'

'I didn't use the word *beautiful* so...'

Never had Alewyn wanted to punch his friend so hard.

'Stop mocking him, Theo,' Benedictus growled. 'Alewyn has done well.' His brother turned to face him. 'I am very pleased with how you have dealt with this mission. I shall mention it to the King. I am sure he will want to reward you in some way.'

Alewyn could only stare at Benedictus. Finally, after all these years, he was hearing approval from the leader of the King's Knights. It validated his place in the elite group and it was all he had ever wanted. Recognition from the King would undoubtedly please his parents and add prestige to their already distinguished lineage. Why then, did he not feel elated?

Chapter Fifteen

Al had been gone for ten days. Winter had finally lessened its hold on the country and the first signs of spring were beginning to make themselves known. Normally, the lengthening days filled Johanne with hope for the year ahead. This year, the mild mornings with their chattering birdsong filled her with dread. The warmer the weather, the more likely Morcant would go ahead with his siege. It didn't matter how much food was stocked in Brae's stores or how many weapons she and her people made, she couldn't help but feel they were headed towards disaster.

When Al had been here, she'd been hopeful. With his strength and organisation she had believed in the impossible. Now he was gone that hope had gradually drained away.

Throughout every long day without him she convinced herself she was fine alone. In the cold, dark hours of the night, she weakened. She realised she did need him, not just for his physical strength but also as someone with whom she could share her burdens, someone to whom she could talk. She had told him she was not interested in marriage. He had left. She needed to learn to live with her decision.

This morning, she had made the rounds of her castle once more. Her people had greeted her happily. For now, they were content. Everything was in place; there was nothing they could do now except wait and practise the drills Al had set them. She could do nothing except praise and encourage her people.

She stopped in the centre of the courtyard. It was looking smarter these days, although she had no wealth left to pay for any more repairs. It seemed her people were taking it upon themselves to keep the place more orderly, something else for which she could thank Al. She climbed the steps above the gatehouse. Gemel was there, eyes focused on the distance.

'Any sign of anything?' she asked as she always did.

'Nothing,' he replied. The same as always.

She stood next to him and stared towards the distant treeline. 'Perhaps we should send a spy into Morcant's territory. Then we would know what was happening.'

'Whom would we send? And before you say yourself, remember that you are needed here.' This was not a new conversation. They were going round in endless loops, each day covering the same ground as if they were stuck on the same spiral staircase, forever going up but never reaching the top.

'We could send Thomas. He is young and fast.' Even as she said it, her heart hurt at the thought. Thomas was keen and desperate for action but he was so young, barely even past childhood.

'I think we are going to have to.' Johanne turned to Gemel in surprise; this was new.

'Do you really think so?'

'We have to do something. We are living on a knife edge. Your people are putting on a good show for you but everyone is tense. Someone is going to snap soon and I'm worried it might be you.'

Gemel was right. Every day it felt as if she were being wound tighter and tighter. They needed information and they needed it now.

'Very well. I will speak to Thomas.' She continued to stare out to the horizon, not moving towards the steps. She could barely admit it to herself but she was not only looking for Morcant but for a solitary rider. A large man, returning to her. It was a foolish daydream. One in which she should stop indulging. Al had returned to his own life. He was not coming back.

Thomas returned that evening, white-faced and trembling.

'He did not have time to go all the way to Morcant's territory,' said Gemel as Thomas approached them.

Johanne's heart pounded. 'No. He did not.'

'What is it, boy?' she asked, although she already knew the answer.

'Morcant's on the move.'

She swallowed. 'And...?'

'He is travelling with many armed men and a weapon.' Thomas stretched his arms above his head and waved them around. 'It is tall. Much bigger than a man, much bigger than several men standing on top of one another.'

'A trebuchet,' said Gemel.

Johanne's stomach twisted. She remembered

the way the trebuchet had loomed high above her and the terror she had experienced when she had first laid eyes on it. It seemed her and Al's efforts had only slowed Morcant down, they had not stopped him. Brae's walls had been reinforced but they would not withstand an attack of this nature. A spark of hope that had flamed ever since Al had set fire to the weapon slowly died. In its place came a new resolve. One she knew would be hard but right.

'Round everyone up and ask them to congregate in the Great Hall immediately,' she said to Gemel. 'I have a message for them. Good lad, Thomas. You have served me well.'

She strode away from the two men. This was it. This was the moment she had dreaded since Badon had died. Her authority was being threatened, but it had not come from within. Her people had been loyal to her to the end. She should have had more faith in herself from the beginning. Al had been right when he said she did not need to hold herself apart from them. Even when doing so, she had created a home for people, a home she could be proud of. Now it was time to let it go.

She strode to Cineas's chamber. He was playing with some wooden horses, his nursemaid by his side. She crouched down beside him. 'My love.'

'Mama.' His smile warmed her heart.

'You are going to go on a journey.'

His eyes widened. 'I am? Will I see Al again?'

She had forgotten how fascinated Cineas had been with Al. She had not spoken his name since he had left. Not even to herself in the quiet of the night when she longed for him the most.

'Not right now, my love. Al is busy doing something for the King.'

That only caused Cineas's eyes to shine brighter. 'Do you think he will bring King Edward to Brae so that he can meet us?'

Oh, how was this so hard? Trying to explain to a little boy that while he was the centre of her world, he was only an acquaintance to Al, someone the knight had met on one of his many missions. Al may already have forgotten Cineas's existence. Now was not the time to introduce Cineas to the realities of the world. 'Maybe another time. Right now, you are going to travel to my brother's home. Remember, I have told you of your uncle.'

Cineas frowned. 'Are you not coming?'

'Not now, my love. But I will follow along later.' God willing.

For the first time, Cineas's excitement dimmed. 'But I want you to be with me.'

'I want it too. But I have things I need to do here. Some of your friends will be coming with you. It will be an adventure. Come here.' She pulled him into an embrace, hoping that he would not notice the tears which dripped into his hair. Please let this not be the last time she held him. 'Be well behaved for your nurse and remember who you are. You are my son but you are also the Baron of Brae. Never forget that.'

He frowned up at her, confused by her uncharacteristic behaviour. If she never saw him again, she hoped he would remember her last words to him, hoped that he would one day claim his birthright.

She left Cineas and his nursemaid packing for the journey and headed to her private chambers. Her people were beginning to gather in the Great Hall and she didn't have long. She pulled out her ledger and tore out a page, cringing at the waste as she did so. For a moment, she was at a loss as to what to say. Her brother was a selfish creature and did nothing for anyone unless it in some way benefitted him. How to appeal to a side of him she wasn't sure existed and ask him to take in her women and children.

In the corner of the room was a wooden box. It contained the small amount of jewellery belonging to the Baroness of Brae. Johanne had never worn it for herself. Badon had not seemed to think her a good enough vessel for such treasures. Since his death, she had only looked at them once. They were not to her taste and so she had decided to keep them for Cineas's wife, who could wear them or melt them down as she so pleased. Now, she would have to use them to pay for Cineas's protection.

She wrapped the box and the letter in a blanket, tucked them under her arm and paused. Should she burn her ledger? If Morcant took control of Brae, she did not want him to have any advantage. He would have to work to make Brae profitable for him. As she stood staring at it, she couldn't help but remember the day Al had come to her. It was the first time they had spoken alone since she had questioned him after he had woken.

She laughed softly to herself. She should have questioned him deeper. He had been lying

to her then. Or had he? She had assumed that
he had lost his memory but, at that stage, he
had not confirmed if he had or not; he had
merely gone along with her assumption.

He was a terrible liar. She could see that
now. He had been so uneasy whenever she had
touched upon his past. If she had been paying proper attention, if she had not been so
focused on what he could do for her, then she
would have realised what he was up to much
earlier on. She was glad she had not done so.
He would have left much sooner and she would
not have got to know him.

God, how she missed him. She missed that
half-smile, his quiet reassurance and—she had
to be honest with herself—she missed watching him as he worked. The way his strength
rippled out from him, the way he could pick up
a log and make it look like a twig. The way he
had lifted her body as if she weighed nothing
and the way he had made it sing.

If he were here right now, would he try and
take control away from her? Probably not. He
had not once done that, not even when the truth
had emerged and it was apparent he was far
above her in rank and wealth. Had she been
foolish to tell him that she didn't need or want

a man in her life? She wasn't sure. Even now, she didn't want to belong to a man again but perhaps together they could have found another way. Maybe marriage didn't have to be about who was the most dominant. Maybe they could have found a way which suited them both. She shook her head. Al had never suggested that he would leave his life as a member of the King's Knights. Even if she had asked him to stay with her, the answer probably would have been no and to leave Brae was not something she could do.

Al needed to prove to himself that he was good enough to belong to the elite group of warrior knights and, until he did that, he would not be able to give himself fully to another person. She could not compete with the life the King could give him.

There was nothing she could do about it now. She would have to live with her decisions and assume that she had done the right thing. To question herself was not constructive.

She took one last look at the ledger and left it where it was. There would be time to destroy it later. For now, she would live in hope.

Chapter Sixteen

Morcant's men came into view in the afternoon of the following day.

They were moving very slowly, the trebuchet being pulled along by several horses.

'It's big,' she croaked to Gemel.

'I thought you'd seen it before.'

'Yes, but this close to Brae's walls it looks even more formidable.'

As the line of men approached, her own people fanned out along the length of the battlements. In the end, only the very young children had left with their mothers. Everyone else had stayed to help. Stocks of arrows were piled high along the wall. Behind her, a fire began to burn, ready to heat up water to throw over their enemy.

As Morcant moved closer, it was apparent

just how large his force was. Johanne's knees began to shake. The inhabitants of Brae may well be enthusiastic, but they could not withstand this barrage.

'Everybody, hold your fire,' she called out. 'We will see what Morcant has to say first.'

There was a muted grumbling among her men, who were more than ready for violence, but everyone obeyed her and held still.

Beneath them, Morcant separated from his men and rode a little forward.

'Lady Johanne,' he called up to her. 'It does not need to come to a battle between us. If you renounce your betrothal and agree to a marriage alliance with me, this will all go away.'

This was the sensible approach. Her people would not die. With the threat of the trebuchet in front of them, marriage was the only way to save them. She opened her mouth to respond but one of her men shouted, 'Never.' And the rest of her people jeered in agreement. Even from this distance, Johanne could see Morcant's lips thin. A bubble of laughter nearly escaped, but she held it in. He did not wait for her own response. 'On your heads be it.'

Morcant wheeled around and began to shout orders at his men. His words were lost in the wind but his intent was clear. The siege was about to begin.

Johanne closed her eyes and leant back against the stone wall behind her. If these were to be her last moments on earth, then she wanted to think of something pleasant. She tried to conjure up images of her son but the thought of him alone in the world without her only made her want to cry.

Instead, she pulled up the memory of Al, his half-smile, his strong but tender hands. She wished she could tell him that she loved him. He deserved to know. She wished she could tell him that she would have liked him in her life. Not to dominate him or for him to dominate her but as a friend and an equal. She wished she had given him the option of staying with her or returning to the knights.

'Johanne.' Gemel's voice stirred her from her imaginings. 'Something is happening.'

She didn't want to open her eyes, didn't want to see the trebuchet being loaded with boulders to be flung at them.

'Johanne. You need to see this.' Gemel sounded excited.

She opened her eyes and then rubbed them. 'What is that?'

'It's the King's standard.'

'What?'

Excited murmurings ran down the battlements as her people leaned over the edge to get a better view at another large group of men approaching Brae.

Morcant's men were not moving; nothing was being loaded into the trebuchet. Morcant was also watching this unexpected approach.

A large group of armed men had formed behind Morcant's. There was something different about them; the way they held themselves in contrast to Morcant's army showed more confidence. They moved in a tight formation and their armour glinted in the sun.

A man who could only be the King rode forward, flanked by four giant men. One of whom towered over the rest. Her heart swelled at the sight of Al, resplendent in his knight's armour. Gemel grabbed hold of her arm and she realised she'd been about to run to him, regardless of the danger below. But oh, how she wanted to go to him. How she wanted to talk to him and to hear his voice in return.

The King and his knights continued to move until they were between Brae and Morcant's men. Johanne wanted to keep her eyes on Al but she knew she needed to concentrate. Whatever was about to happen was vitally important for Brae's future.

Johanne leaned over the edge of the battlements in order to hear what was being said. Her movement caused Al to turn in his saddle. He glanced up at her and his mouth tilted in her favourite half-smile. Her stomach fluttered and she smiled back.

'What is the meaning of this?' bellowed the King.

There was only silence. Morcant looked like a sulky boy who'd been caught stealing apples. Johanne couldn't help the laugh that escaped her, causing the King and the rest of his knights to turn to face her. King Edward leaned over and muttered something to Al, who nodded. The King turned to her. 'Lady Johanne. Perhaps you will join us.'

It was difficult to tell from his voice whether the King was angry or pleased with her. Recognising that his statement was not a request but an order, she turned and ran down to the castle gates. The portcullis took an age to rise. Her heart was fluttering wildly and she knew this was not because she was going to meet the King. She had truly believed she would never see Al again and now she would be close to him once more.

She burst into the light and came to a stop before King Edward's horse. She squinted up at him as the sun glinted off his armour. Collecting herself, she bowed her head before him. She looked up and caught Al's amused half-smile.

'Lady Johanne, it is a pleasure to meet you. I understand you were crucial in uncovering a plot against the Crown.'

'I…' She glanced at Al, who nodded slightly. 'Thank you.' Her response made little sense, but King Edward did not seem to notice.

'As a thank-you for your work, Castle Brae is being granted the King's protection.' King Edward turned back to Morcant. 'I am not sure what is going on here but, know this, any enemy of Lady Johanne is an enemy of mine. If you attack Brae today, then my men will be forced to retaliate.' The King's gaze flicked over Morcant's assembled men. Next to the King's, they looked very bedraggled. They would not be able to fight the King's army and live to tell the tale. Towards the back of Morcant's group, men were already disappearing into the forest beyond, not willing to risk their lives now they knew they were up against a superior fighting force.

Johanne kept herself very still. She could hardly believe what was happening in front of her; it was as if she were dreaming and yet she could feel the sun on her back and a slight breeze playing with her hair. She turned to Al. He was gazing directly at her, not paying the slightest bit of attention to Morcant. She stepped towards him when King Edward spoke again.

'You will leave here and never bother Lady Johanne again.' Johanne turned back to see Morcant nod weakly. She swallowed another laugh. 'I am going to leave some of my men here to make sure you understand these new rules. You may leave now.'

Morcant turned to his men. 'You heard the King.'

'You can leave the trebuchet.' The King's voice boomed out across the space. For a moment it looked as if Morcant might argue, but after a quick glance at the King's army, he changed his mind.

With one final glare for Johanne, Morcant turned to go. Johanne didn't stop to watch.

She ran to Al's horse just as he jumped down from it.

'You came.'

He laughed. 'Of course. We cut it a little fine but we got the job done. Morcant is a coward at heart. I knew he would not want to battle the King's men. I doubt he will try again but the men left here will ensure your safety.'

'Thank you.'

One of the towering knights leaned over in his saddle. 'The King owed Alewyn a favour and he chose to save Brae. Isn't that—'

'Thank you, Theo. We don't need your input.' Al was frowning up at his friend, who only grinned back.

Al looked back at her. She couldn't tell from the expression on his face whether he was as pleased to see her as she was to see him. 'Asking for the King's favour was the best way to repay you for all you have done for me.'

Oh. Was that why he was here? Because he thought he owed her a debt of gratitude. A spark of hope died. 'Thank you. We were prepared to fight but...' She glanced at Morcant's retreating army. 'We would have lost.'

'I think you should have more faith in yourself. The walls of Brae are looking strong.

Your men are clearly prepared.' He gestured to the castle, but she didn't take her eyes off him. 'Where is Cineas?'

'I sent him to my brother's castle, along with some of the other young children and their mothers.'

'I thought you said your brother did nothing for other people.' Her heart squeezed that he'd remembered such a small detail about her. There was so much she wanted to say but that knight was still looking at them, an amused smirk across his face. 'I sent him some of the Baroness of Brae's jewellery so—'

'We must make haste.' A stern man with thick, black eyebrows broke into their conversation. 'Now that the King has made himself known in this part of the country, we cannot risk word getting to Yonescu.' The man looked between the two of them. 'Have you finished here?'

Johanne held her breath.

'Yes,' said Al, nodding to the other man, who had to be his brother. They had the same thick, dark hair. 'We're finished.' Johanne's heart pounded painfully against her ribs. 'It was good to see you again, Lady Johanne. The men the King is leaving with you are excellent fighters; I trained them myself. They will stay for a month. After that, should you have any problems with Morcant send word to the King. He is an honourable man and if he has promised that Brae is under the protection of the Crown, then he means it.'

Johanne knew she should be concentrating on this. It was the sort of information dreams were made of and yet all she could think of was that her moment with Al was coming to an end and she couldn't find the words to tell him all the things she'd been thinking since he'd left: how much he meant to her and how much she wanted him to be a part of her life. The man with the dark eyebrows was glaring down at her. The words in her throat died. She couldn't tell Al that she loved him while he was surrounded by men who might tear her words down, who would probably make him choose a different path. She glanced down at her chest, surprised to see it wasn't visibly bleeding.

And Al was saying nothing either. If he had given any hint that he wanted to stay with her or that he would welcome her words of love, then perhaps she would be braver. But no... 'Thank you,' was all she said in the end.

Al nodded. 'Good day, Lady Johanne.'

'Good day,' she managed weakly.

As quickly as they had come, King Edward, his knights and his army left, leaving Johanne safe from physical harm but not from the hurt in her heart.

Chapter Seventeen

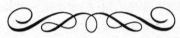

'**Y**ou're an idiot.'

Alewyn didn't even turn to look at Theo; he couldn't bear to. Every time his friend spoke it took all that Alewyn had not to push him off his horse. 'That's the third time you've told me so in the last two leagues. I'm enjoying it less every time you say it.'

'I will keep saying it until you pay attention.'

Alewyn tightened his grip on the reins. 'I have paid attention. In your opinion, I should have abandoned my oath, confessed my undying love to Jo… Lady Johanne and stayed at Brae,' he said dryly. 'Aside from the fact that the lady has made it very clear she does not want me in her life, I'm fairly sure that course of action counts as treasonous and, if I followed it, would result in me being locked up at best and hanged at worst.'

Theo rode up so that he was alongside. Alewyn still didn't look at him. 'I think you should have told the beautiful woman running towards you with her heart in her eyes that you loved her and that you would be back as soon as you had dealt with Yonescu. You do love her, don't you?'

Alewyn muttered a curse under his breath.

'I thought as much. You should have told her.'

Alewyn snorted. 'I just told you, she doesn't want me. Not like that.'

'Oh, so how does she want you exactly?'

Alewyn turned his head away so that Theo could not see his face at all. He knew he wouldn't be able to hide the expression on his face when he thought about the two nights he had spent in her bed. Nothing in his life had ever compared, even slightly, to the joy and pleasure of lying with her. It hadn't been all physical. There had been the moments in between, the moments where they had laughed and talked about everything and nothing. Those were the moments his head kept replaying. The moments where he had been himself, not a knight, not a younger brother or second son. He had been Al, a man with nothing else to do but love the woman he was with. Those moments had been his personal heaven.

'You haven't answered the question.'

Alewyn growled. 'Lady Johanne was very kind to me and, in return, I helped her to secure her castle. She never gave any indication that she wanted me in any other capacity.'

'Are you absolutely sure about that? It seemed to me that she very much wanted you to stay.'

Irritation spiked. 'You're the expert then, on Lady Johanne. A woman you met for a few scant moments.'

Theo cleared his throat. 'I have been known to be able to read people without them speaking, yes.' Damn it all to hell. That was true. Theo was good at that; it was why he was one of the King's elite warriors.

'You were not very good at it with your own wife,' Al countered.

'That's because I was blinded by love. I just didn't know it at the time.' It would help if Theo stopped being reasonable. 'I think the question is, do you love Lady Johanne enough? If you do, then your course of action is simple.'

They rode in silence for a moment. 'All

right, I'll bite. What would be my course of action, if I were in love with her?'

'Marry her. Or at least ask her to marry you.'

Alewyn's heart began to pound. 'It's not that simple. She would not want to leave Brae until her son was in his majority and can take over the running of Brae. My work for the King's Knights takes up most of my time. I could not ask her to live in Windsor with me, her life at Brae is too important to her and I cannot leave the King's Knights.'

'Why not?' asked Theo softly. Alewyn shot a glance at his friend. Theo was not smirking at him. For once, his eyes held compassion. It was harder to argue against. Alewyn turned away but Theo hadn't finished with him.

'You are very much in the King's favour right now. Not only did you uncover Yonescu's plot but the way you defeated those Frenchmen…'

Alewyn found himself smiling for the first time in days. It was true he had overcome the Frenchmen hiding in Cranleigh. He'd been the one to find their hiding place and, fuelled by rage at the thought of these men nearly causing Johanne to hang, he'd had them subdued before anyone else arrived.

'I can't leave the King's Knights because…'
Alewyn stopped. Why couldn't he leave? It
wasn't common but the King did grant permis-
sion to knights he favoured to leave his ranks
and protect their own households. If the King
required them to return to service, then they
had to do so but that was not such an onerous
task. It was not that which was stopping him.

'Well?'

'It has long been an assumption of my family that my brother and I will be part of the
King's court at Windsor. The Monceaux family have been one of leading British families
since William took control in 1066.'

'I understand why you feel you cannot let
your family down. It is natural not to want to
be the disappointing son. For most of my life,
that is how my family saw me and it is surprisingly painful.' Theo was uncharacteristically
serious. 'You need to ask yourself whether
how other people see you really matters to
you, deep down.'

Alewyn thought. Did he really want to live
his life proving to his family that he was worthy of the Monceaux name? Wasn't it about
time he did something that made him happy?
And was that happiness tied up with Johanne
of Brae?

'Well?'

'I thought I was asking myself, not telling you.'

'I would like an answer.'

'I still need time to think.'

He had proven to his brother and to himself that he was worthy of his place in the King's Knights but that had not given him the satisfaction he expected. It had not made him feel as good as helping Johanne secure Brae had done. His fellow knights were his brothers, but since he had returned to their fold, he had not laughed, had not felt the intense achievement of a job well done, had not felt his heart pound with the joy of being close to someone he loved.

'Well?'

'I'm going to end you.'

Theo laughed. 'You are a brave man, Alewyn. Courageous in a way I have never seen in anyone else. Do you have it in yourself to make the bravest decision of your life?'

Alewyn didn't answer.

Johanne sat staring at her open ledger; she could hear the distant shrieks of children's laughter as they played in the courtyard. Life

at Brae had been one long celebration since
Morcant's men had been sent away. The men
who had been left by the King to protect Brae
had fitted in well with the rest of her people
and she wouldn't be surprised if at least two
of them requested to stay as romance seemed
to be blossoming with some of her women. It
would give her more able-bodied men, which
is what she'd wanted. Cineas was safe and
so was his legacy. She should be happy. The
smiles she pasted on her face whenever she
was around her people never came from her
heart. Sometimes, she was surprised it was
still beating; it felt so heavy.

'Do you have everything you need?'

'Yes, thank you, Gemel.' She smiled at her
steward. She was trying to be more open, to let
go of the barriers Alewyn had pointed out she
always wore around herself. For the most part,
she was winning. She was letting her people
see the real her and they had responded well.
She had told no one of her deepest secret: her
devastation at losing Al. She had told everyone
that they had decided to end their betrothal because of Al's commitment to the King. No one
had questioned her and hardly anyone mentioned his name in front of her, for which she

was grateful. She wanted him so much. In the darkness of the night, when she was so alone it hurt so badly it was as if she were bleeding internally.

'Why don't you send a messenger to him?'

Johanne looked up sharply. 'Who?'

Gemel raised a bushy eyebrow.

She sighed. She *had* gone so far as to consider travelling to Windsor and asking to see Al, to tell him how she loved him and wanted him with her and to hell with the consequences. That desire normally came to her in the middle of the night and was not something she would admit to Gemel. There was a limit to how much sharing she could do. Besides, the light of the morning always brought a calmer reflection.

'Al was the one who left, Gemel. If he'd wanted to stay, then he would have done so. I am not going to chase after him. He would be bored here at Brae.' If he'd wanted to be with her, he would have reiterated his comments about marriage when she last saw him. He had not. Instead, he had spoken of his obligation and then ridden out of her life without a backward glance. Again. He had barely been with her a moment before he had returned to his true calling in life. He had not seemed sad to leave her.

'Perhaps, you could—'

'Thank you, Gemel, for all your support. I know that you are being kind but, please, I do not want to talk about it anymore.'

Gemel nodded slowly. 'Very well. I shall leave you to your ledger. Don't stay in here all day. The weather is lovely and there is talk of the young ones putting on a play.'

She smiled and nodded. She would make an effort not to miss that. Most days, the children of the castle were the only reason she managed to keep going.

She tried to concentrate on her columns of figures but the numbers wouldn't stay where she wanted them. Gemel bringing Al up meant that she could no longer think of anything else. It was no good. She would have to learn to live without him. It shouldn't be that hard. She hadn't known him that long. The pain of missing him would surely fade soon. It had to; she couldn't go on feeling this level of dark misery for much longer.

'Mama, look who's here.'

Johanne looked up at Cineas's words and then blinked, trying to dispel the image before her, the sight of Al standing in the door frame, his body taking up the whole space. It couldn't be real. It was because she had been thinking about him so intensely. But Cineas was tugging him forward, his tiny hand in Al's massive one, his whole body vibrating with happiness.

She stood slowly. 'Al.'

'Johanne.' Al allowed Cineas to bring him into the room all the while keeping his gaze on her face. She touched her throat where her pulse beat erratically.

'What…? Why…?' It dawned on her that he might not be here to see her. She willed her heart to stop racing. 'Are you here to collect the King's men? They have been very helpful but I suppose Edward will be wanting them back. Do you think he will allow any of them to stay? Only I think some of them have formed attachments. Was your mission to arrest Yonescu successful? Is his operation disbanded? Have—'

His lips curled in his delicious half-smile. 'Do you ever stop asking questions?'

She couldn't help but smile back. 'Only when they are answered.'

He laughed. 'No, I am not here to collect any

men on Edward's behalf. He said they would stay for a month, and he will keep his word. Edward may let some of them stay, although they will be required to come to France, should war break out. They will have to petition him. He is in a generous mood because, yes, the operation to capture Yonescu was successful and all the Frenchmen who entered the country have been arrested.'

'I didn't see the King when he came. I went to see my uncle and I missed his arrival.' Cineas pulled a face showing just how little he had enjoyed that trip. 'Mama says I cannot ask you to take me to Windsor so that I can see him but I don't understand why. You will take me, won't you, Al?'

'Cineas…' Neither of them looked in her direction.

Al smiled. 'Yes. Of course I will take you. I am sure he will be very pleased to meet the Baron of Brae.'

Cineas jumped up and down on his toes. 'When can we leave?'

Al laughed. 'Not right now.' He crouched down so he was on a level with Cineas. 'I need to talk to your mama. I have things to say that are private. I will come and find you when I am finished and we will talk about visiting Windsor some more.'

For a moment, it looked as if Cineas would argue but excitement at sharing his news overcame him and he rushed out of the chamber without a second glance.

'Al. That is kind of you to offer to take him to visit the King but, please, I do not expect you to do that. Besides, I do not think I could be parted from him again so soon. It was hard when he went to my brother's stronghold and...' Her words petered out. How to explain that if she could not have Al for herself, it would be too hard to keep seeing him, for him to come in and out of her life.

'I was hoping,' Al said quietly, 'that I would be able to take both of you. Not to stay, but to visit. That we could go as a family of three.'

When she didn't say anything, he moved around the desk and leant on the edge of it next to her seat. She leaned forward, unable to stop herself from lightly touching the back of his hand. He turned his palm outwards and laced his fingers with hers.

'Johanne, I'm here because...' He swallowed. 'I realised I never told you that I love you and I think that's something you should know.'

She stared up at him, her words, for once, abandoning her. She'd only hoped that she could see him again; she'd never believed, even for the smallest of moments, that he would tell her that he loved her. That he'd want her and Cineas to be part of his family.

Al squeezed her hand. 'Say something.' Still her words wouldn't come. 'Even a barrage of questions would be welcome at this point.'

'I…' She stood, making sure to keep her fingers intertwined with his. 'I love you too.' She leaned forward and pressed her lips to his.

For an endless moment, they stood like this. Their lips moving over each other. She was content just to hold him, to finally be with him after so long apart. After a while, he lifted his head. 'I know that you don't want to marry again. I understand that Badon was a cruel and indifferent husband but a union between us would be different. I would not want to control you. I would only want to work with you, to create a home that is safe and true to its inhabitants. A place that is full of laughter.'

She swallowed. 'What of your role amongst the King's Knights?'

He inhaled deeply. 'I have requested and been granted the right to leave the King's Knights.'

She couldn't speak, couldn't move for the sheer shock of his statement.

'Say something.'

'I... But... I thought your whole mission was to prove you warrant your place in the King's Knights. You discovered Yonescu's plot so I don't understand...'

Al shrugged. 'All my life I have not felt worthy of my prestigious family name and my place in the King's elite warriors. I undertook the mission desperate to prove my value and, when I did, I realised it didn't matter. Benedictus has taken me leaving very badly. I'm sure the rest of my family will not be pleased either, but I realised that what my parents think of me, what my brother and my King believe me capable of, does not compare with the simple joy of being with you. Hey...' He wiped the tears from her cheeks. 'I did not mean to make you cry.'

'I never thought... I never believed that you would want to stay with me, here at Brae.'

'And now that I do...?' He leaned his forehead against hers.

'I want you here with me more than any-thing.' His lips grazed hers. 'But will it be enough for you? Sieges and treasonous plots do not normally happen around here. Life will be dull in comparison to what you are used to.'

His lips curved in his familiar half-smile and her heart took flight. 'Life with you will never be boring. That I can guarantee. I love you, Lady Johanne. Please will you do me the greatest honour and be my wife, my friend and my equal?'

'Yes. I will.' And that was the last either of them said for some time.

* * * * *

COMING SOON!

We really hope you enjoyed reading this book. If you're looking for more romance, be sure to head to the shops when new books are available on

Thursday 29th September

To see which titles are coming soon, please visit

millsandboon.co.uk/nextmonth

MILLS & BOON®

Coming next month

HIS CONVENIENT DUCHESS
Louise Allen

'Miss Wrayford, perhaps we could talk privately.'

She looked a little surprised at his interruption but said readily, 'Why, yes. Shall we go into the morning room?'

He gave a little nod and followed her across the hall and into the pleasant, sunny room. A sewing box stood open on the table and beside it was a pile of folded linen garments. She saw his glance and chuckled as she walked towards the table

'I stand upon no ceremony with you, sir and shall not apologise for the signs of industry you see here. I have been mending some of Toby's shirts. It always amazes me how Betty can send him out looking like a little gentleman and he returns like a ragamuffin!'

Winning no answering smile from him, her amusement faded and she looked a little puzzled.

'How may I help you, Mr Devereux?'

Leo carefully placed his hat and gloves on a side table.

'It is time for me to tell you the truth, Miss Wrayford.' He turned to face her. 'My name is Leopold John Hugo Devereux de Quinton.'

Oh?' She looked even more bewildered.

'I am Duke of Tain.'

The name meant nothing to her. That much was clear from the way her eyes widened with innocent surprise.

'Why should a duke be masquerading as a commoner?'

'Alice never mentioned me to you?'

'Alice? No, why should she…'

He saw the look of horror dawning in her eyes and spoke quickly.

'I am Toby's father.'

She put out a hand, groping for the chairback.

'No!' she whispered. 'No. That cannot be.'

She sank down onto the chair, all the while keeping her gaze fixed upon him. He looked away.

'Yesterday I received the correspondence from my lawyers. There can be no doubt that Toby is my son and I have the papers to prove it.'

She clasped her hands in her lap, the knuckles gleaming bone white beneath the skin.

'Will you explain why are you here now?' she asked him. 'Why you have shown up after all these years?'

Continue reading
HIS CONVENIENT DUCHESS
Louise Allen

Available next month
www.millsandboon.co.uk

MILLS & BOON

THE HEART OF ROMANCE

A ROMANCE FOR EVERY READER

MODERN

Prepare to be swept off your feet by sophisticated, sexy and seductive heroes, in some of the world's most glamourous and romantic locations, where power and passion collide.

HISTORICAL

Escape with historical heroes from time gone by. Whether your passion is for wicked Regency Rakes, muscled Vikings or rugged Highlanders, awaken the romance of the past.

MEDICAL

Set your pulse racing with dedicated, delectable doctors in the high-pressure world of medicine, where emotions run high and passion, comfort and love are the best medicine.

True Love

Celebrate true love with tender stories of heartfelt romance, from the rush of falling in love to the joy a new baby can bring, and a focus on the emotional heart of a relationship.

Desire

Indulge in secrets and scandal, intense drama and plenty of sizzling hot action with powerful and passionate heroes who have it all: wealth, status, good looks…everything but the right woman.

HEROES

Experience all the excitement of a gripping thriller, with an intense romance at its heart. Resourceful, true-to-life women and strong, fearless men face danger and desire - a killer combination!

To see which titles are coming soon, please visit

millsandboon.co.uk/nextmonth